# ASTER WOOD

## AND THE

## CHILD OF ELYSO

Cover art by Ken Tan

Special thanks to Zoe Strickland

# CHAPTER ONE

I hit hard.

My bare arms scraped against short, dead cornstalks as I skidded across the field, finally coming to a stop in a cloud of dust. A mouthful of bone dry dirt choked me, and I coughed. My eyes watered as a cold wind blew against my face. I stared around.

I was home.

My heart sank.

Everything was the same as before. Stark. Vast. Dead.

I hadn't expected to feel anything other than joy at returning, finally, to Earth. But the barren landscape was a shock, something I hadn't seen in many long months, and it did not welcome me. No breathtaking vistas awaited. No gently trickling streams. No warm sunlight beneath teal skies. Compared to the planets in the Triaden, it seemed nothing of beauty remained in this place.

My fists dug into the loose, gravelly dirt, and I pushed myself up to standing. The scrapes on my arms stung, but they would heal. The coughing gradually ceased. I rubbed the dirt out of my stinging eyes.

I was in Adams county. I knew that, even though I had spent most of my childhood in the city. I recognized the odd rock formations to the east, with the telltale shapes I had gazed upon since early childhood. Somewhere out here was Grandma's farm. I spun around, searching the brown, lifeless horizon. Overhead, storm clouds threatened.

Cait burst through, landing nearly as hard as I had. Her little body rolled over and over like a carelessly thrown doll, bumping and scraping along the ground. She cried out with a particularly rough thump to the knees and tumbled to a stop just a few feet away.

I rushed in her direction, my temporary disappointment immediately replaced with worry for the little girl.

"Cait," I huffed, my throat still choked with dust. "Are you okay?"

Her giant blue eyes looked into mine for a quick moment, her face frozen with a look of shock. Then, the corners of her mouth turned down. She whimpered.

"Owie," she said, her mouth opening wide into a silent cry, fat tears dripping down her dirty cheeks.

She unfolded her legs from beneath her and inspected them. At the sight of the blood on her knees, she cried louder. Suddenly, her eyes became frightened, and I noticed her shrink away from me as I got closer. She had trusted me. She hadn't counted on scraped knees. That hadn't been part of the deal.

"Cait, it's alright," I said, kneeling down. I moved one hand out to inspect her leg, but she snatched the injury away. I paused, thinking, then sat down in the dirt beside her. "You'll be okay," I said, trying to employ the same soothing sound my mother used to when I would get hurt as a young child. "It's just a couple of scrapes. It'll heal fast. Are you hurt anywhere else?"

She ventured a look in my direction, sniffed hard, then shook her head. The tears still came, but they were silent now.

"Good," I said. "Now, I told you I'm going to take care of you, remember?"

She stared.

"We're on Earth now," I continued. "Everything's going to be better here. The Coyle," I paused, not wanting to upset her further. "He can't get to you here. Do you understand?"

She didn't respond, but she didn't shy away again. Another blast of winter wind hit us, and we both shivered.

"Come on," I said, standing up and reaching out both my hands to her. "It's not going to get any warmer. Let's start walking."

I pulled out the traveling cloak from my pack and draped it over both of us. Instantly, the wind was blocked as though we had our own little room to protect us from it. It had been Kiron's gift to me when I had first met him, and the cloak had kept me warm through much more severe elements than these.

As Cait and I took our first steps away from our landing spot, I bent and scooped up the chaser she had used to follow me here, stuffing the fat ball into my pocket.

"Better?" I asked, tucking the blanket back around us again.

She looked up, eyes round, and nodded.

"Can you walk?"

Another nod.

Guessing that we were northwest of the farm, we started off, the hills on our left side. It was difficult to tell the time of day with the cloud cover, morning or afternoon, but the fact that it was still light at all was comforting. As much traveling as I had done at night in the Fold, something about the idea of walking around on my own planet in the dark made me nervous. There may not be evil wizards on Earth, but there were other, less obvious perils.

My first days in the Triaden seemed like years ago now. Was it possible that only eight months ago I had been a sick, weak kid? My ailing heart had cursed me since birth, and only upon arriving at Kiron's doorstep had I found the magic, and the will, to heal. I had journeyed so far since then, met wizards and demons and fought battles that the people of Earth would never have believed. Eventually, I discovered my own unique sort of magic, tied to the vibrance of life that pulsed in the Maylin Fold and my tendency to find hope within the most dire circumstances.

But that magic wasn't with me here. I had left my wood staff, the vehicle that brought my power to life, with Kiron and the others. They would need every weapon they could get to fight the Corentin and his armies in my absence.

And they would fight Jade, too, I realized. To fight the enemy would be to fight the girl I had met and befriended at the very start of my travels in the Fold. The girl, my own flesh and blood, who had eventually fallen to the possession of the Corentin. She had tried to kill me more than once since then. And yet I still felt that feeling, that tiny spark of hope that someday I could free her from the prison the Corentin had created for her within her mind.

I picked up the pace as I thought of her, of my friends facing off against her. I hoped I could find the gold I needed on Earth and return before another drop of blood was shed. Before any more of my friends fell victim to the Corentin, or his minion, the Coyle. Time was running out.

Our feet crunched through the dead stalks as we walked. Cait's eyes drifted around, and I could tell she was concerned about where her path had taken her. I couldn't blame her. Between the biting wind and the expanse of dead fields, it was not a friendly looking place.

"Things used to be different here," I said, looking across the fields, myself. "Before I was born, this place was a lot like Aeso."

She looked up hopefully, as though the landscape might change back to the familiar green of her homeland with my story. I continued.

"I never saw it, though. Only pictures."

"What's pictures?" she asked.

It was the first time she had really spoken. But I didn't know what to say. *What's pictures?* I chewed on the inside of my cheek, thinking. Of course she wouldn't know. They might have wizards and magic in the Fold, but we had our own kind of magic on Earth. We called it *technology.*

"Have you ever made a drawing?" I finally asked. "Or a painting? Like with a paintbrush?"

She nodded.

"Then you've made a picture before," I said. "You draw a picture. You paint a picture. Only the types of pictures I'm talking about are made a different way, with something called a camera."

She looked confused.

I sighed.

"It's sort of hard to explain," I continued. "You use the camera, and you take the picture."

"Where do you take it?" she asked.

I stopped, staring at her, and then suddenly burst out laughing.

"No, no," I said. "You don't take it anywhere. The word take is like the word paint. It's like, you make the picture."

She looked down, seemingly embarrassed by my laughter.

"I'm not laughing at you," I said, backpedaling. I put one hand on her shoulder, squeezing. We walked on. "It's just hard to explain. Anyways, you take the picture, and it's kind of like drawing with a brush. But what comes out has more detail than a painting." I looked up towards the distant hills, remembering. "It's almost like having a memory that you can hold in your hands and look at with your eyes."

She was silent.

"I'll show you when we get there," I said, feeling a little defeated.

"Where are we going?" she asked. Her little moccassined foot kicked against the dry stalks as we walked.

"To my grandmother's house," I said. "My father's mother."

"I know what a grandmother is," she said quietly.

I suddenly felt ashamed at having laughed. She was just a little kid, a day and a half out of being possessed by the Coyle. And now this, hurtled to a planet she didn't know or understand.

I stopped walking again, turned to her and knelt down.

"I'm sorry I laughed," I said, looking her in the eye. "I remember feeling just like you when I came to Aerit for the first time. There were lots of things I didn't understand. I felt stupid. And scared. Really scared."

She folded her arms in front of her chest.

"I'm *not* scared," she said stubbornly.

For a moment I was taken aback. Then, without knowing where the understanding came from, I suddenly knew what to say.

"I know you're not scared. You're way tougher than me."

*And you've been through way more.*

"I'm just trying to explain," I went on. "There might be lots of things here that you don't understand right away. So if you see something new, just ask me about it, okay? I promise I won't laugh anymore. Deal?"

She pulled the blanket close around her face, looked up at me with untrusting eyes.

"Tell you what," I said. "Do you want to ride on my back? You remember I'm pretty fast, right?"

I turned my back to her, encouraging her to climb aboard. Suddenly, she smiled.

"Okay," she said, gripping her little arms around my neck.

I stood up and folded her legs into the crooks of my arms, turning to face the direction we had been traveling in. But before I could take a single step, I froze.

A sudden sense of danger overwhelmed me at the idea of running, and my eyes scanned the flat, open land before me. In another life a simple jog might have meant my death. My heart, diseased since birth, had prevented me from accomplishing anything more exciting than a brisk walk for the majority of my life. In all of my thirteen years, the only time I had ever breathed easily, or run fast, was back in the Triaden.

Was my heart, now beating Earth's oxygen into my veins again, still healed?

"Come on," Cait urged, squeezing her legs against my sides as if I were a pony.

I chuckled, trying to push fear away, and took a few tentative steps.

Nothing happened. My heart did not explode in my chest. My breathing was normal.

I pushed a little faster, a slow run now.

My heart beat, strong and steady. My breath came, free and clear.

Could it be possible?

I felt my body launch forward like a truck hitting fifth gear, and suddenly the dirt was flying beneath my feet. Cait squealed with delight at the speed, but I wanted to go faster. My breath came in gasps now, but I didn't care. I pushed my legs harder. And harder.

But the blinding speed I was searching for eluded me.

I focused on a point on the horizon, willing my body to shoot towards it like a bullet from a gun. My feet hit one after the other, again and again until I was running with all the efficiency of one of Earth's machines.

But I could not go faster.

Finally, I slowed, first to a jog, then a walk. I stopped, panting hard, releasing Cait from my back. She slid down to the ground, her hair a mess, a huge smile on her face.

"That was fun," she said. "You're faster than Rhainn-y."

I smiled back. But inside, my heart hurt. Not from the effort of the run, but from my lack of speed. I had run fast, that was sure. But nowhere near as fast as I could in the Fold.

My ability to run was the only piece of magic I had known since the moment my feet touched the ground on Aerit, Kiron's home planet. I had left the staff with Kiron, believing that its magic wouldn't work on Earth. But part of me had hoped that I was wrong, that somewhere within Earth magic stirred, and I would still have the uncanny ability to run faster than any animal that had ever traversed these lands.

I leaned over as I caught my breath. Sweat broke out over my body, and I shivered as my skin met the cold air.

There was no magic here. It had been as I had believed. Any magic Earth contained, it seemed, was as dead as the plains surrounding us.

But I was still healthy. Still strong. The lack of obvious power was not a death sentence.

Standing back up again, I put my hands on my hips and looked down at Cait.

"Maybe we should walk for a while," I said.

"No!" she said. "Again! Again!"

I smiled.

"In a little while, okay?"

"Awww," she complained. But she fell into step beside me as I started walking again.

I slid my hand beneath my shirt, holding it over my chest. I could feel my heart beating beneath my fingers. It felt strong. New. The breath I sucked in and out of my lungs was clear. My chest did not clench.

I was healed, it seemed, both on Earth and in the Fold. But the speed I had found, the speed that had protected me, saved me from so many dangerous encounters, was gone. Would it come back to me, the magic I had felt coursing through my veins, when I returned to the Fold? Or did a return to Earth mean that my time as someone extraordinary was over?

I had been brought to the Fold, a crease in the fabric of space that allowed easy travel between planets, by accident. I hadn't known that the blank letter I had held in my hands was actually a link, a portal to a place far from here. Upon arriving I had learned that my ancestors had not come from Earth. That my existence had been, basically, an accident.

But now, with Earth in a state of steep decline, and the three planets that made up the Triaden in the Fold at war with the armies of the Corentin, things had changed. Without my presence, without the accidents that had brought me into being and later sent me hurtling across the cosmos, Earth and all of its inhabitants would have unknowingly met an unimaginable enemy. One who would destroy what was left of Earth beyond imagining. Everything around us that my eyes could make out, the remnants of a society that no longer existed, would be obliterated once Earth became close enough for the Corentin to stretch out his rule and blanket this planet with his darkness. The people who remained, who had survived the Long Drought and made lives for themselves in the towering cities, would have fallen to him as so many others had already.

Others could fight him. Others could make their attempts to restore order to the planets that now swung wildly out of alignment.

But only I could come back here and get them the gold they needed to do it.

I reached out my hand automatically, and Cait took it. Together, our feet crunched through the dead stalks, which had lived only long enough to be disintegrated by the poison rains that now haunted everyone who remained.

We walked for hours. Sometimes side by side, sometimes Cait riding piggyback. Far in the distance a couple of buildings came into view. The sky was growing darker now, either from the day ending or the clouds growing thicker, I couldn't tell. I hoped that one of those buildings up ahead was the farm. There was nowhere to take shelter out here from the cold of a winter night.

Suddenly, the sky seemed to split open. A crack so loud I had to put my hands over my ears as it echoed across the clouds. My stomach dropped painfully. I knew what that sound meant.

Rain.

Cait had her hands over her ears, too, but only for a moment. To her, the rain was nothing more than something unpleasant we would have to walk through. Maybe not even that. She might have even taken delight in splashing through the puddles along the journey. If the journey we were on had been on any other planet but Earth.

She didn't understand.

I knelt down in front of her again.

"Time to get back on, Cait," I said. "Make sure you wrap that blanket around you tight, okay?" She looked confused at the tension in my voice, but she didn't argue.

The sky was darkest behind us, and it was a relief to realize that we wouldn't be running into the rain, but away from it. I took a wild guess that the buildings up ahead were two miles out. How long would it take me to get there in this mortal body?

I broke into a run, immediately winded by my panic.

*Wait. Pace yourself, or you'll never make it.*

I forced myself to slow down. Between my pack and Cait, I had nearly eighty pounds on my back.

The sky cracked again. And again. It was only a matter of time. The clouds were right behind us.

*Be careful. Don't fall.*

I had seen the people who had been caught out in the rain in the hospital when I was a small child, their skin taught and red as though seared with a hot iron. If I fell and twisted an ankle, hit my knees in the dirt the way Cait had, it could be the difference between life and death.

The raindrops started. I felt the first one on the top of my fist, the second on the tip of my nose. The acidic water rested innocently on my flesh for several seconds. Then it began to burn.

"Owww!" Cait yelled from my back, clearly struck, herself. "Owww, it hurts!"

"I know," I called back. "Hang on. Make sure you're covered by the blanket!"

Her cries became howls of pain as I ran through the fields. We had to get there. Had to reach beneath the protection of the old buildings up ahead. I heaved us through the dirt, which was quickly becoming sticky mud.

How long had it been? How far had I come? A half mile? A mile?

The water began to puddle at my feet, and it splashed up around my calves with every stride I took.

I panted, pushing myself to go faster, all the while keeping the buildings up ahead in sight.

Were they getting closer?

Rain made its way into my eyes, and they stung as if I had opened them under ocean waves.

They *were* getting closer. Up ahead, I could see the road, long disused and crumbling. I didn't bother to look for cars as I stumbled across the pavement. There would be no traffic out here. There would be nobody at all.

"Are you okay?" I choked as I ran.

Cait's quiet whimpers of pain seemed to bounce around the inside of my skull.

My face burned. My bare arms felt like they were on fire. Now that we were close, I couldn't tell with my stinging eyes if this was the farm at all. But it was shelter. It was a way out of this pain, and I pushed with everything I had to get us there.

The water seeped through my pants, coating my skin with the sharp sting of acid.

Why had I come? In that moment I wished I had stayed in the Fold. What good could come from returning to a place like this? Earth was ravaged. Destroyed. And now it would destroy us.

The mist that hung in the air was finding its way into my throat, and I coughed. It seared as if I was drinking boiling water.

Cait had gone quiet now, but her fingers gripped hard around my neck. I put my head down, trying to shield my face from the spray. I looked up from time to time, watched the looming farmhouse getting closer and closer.

The rain seemed to sense that our respite was close. The sky opened up and dumped water down upon us. Just steps away from the front porch of the house, I was completely drenched but for the place on my back where Cait's little body was pressed into mine, every other inch of me screaming in agony.

Then we were there. I dropped Cait, hard, on the porch. She came back to life, wailing in pain. I fell to my hands and knees, crawled towards the door, everything blurred and confused. My eyeballs felt like they were melting within their sockets. The handle was locked. I pounded on the wood, praying that someone inside would hear us, would help us.

I slumped down at the doorway, no longer able to summon any strength to fight. Every ounce of energy I had was gone, sapped away from the run, insulted further by the stinging rain. I heard Cait's cries, but I could do nothing for her. I could barely breathe, myself.

The world started to go dark, and I fought off unconsciousness. I had to get us inside. I had to protect Cait. I had promised I would.

Behind me, I heard sounds, muffled by my exhausted brain. The door handle creaked, the wood groaned, and the door to the house opened.

Someone stepped over the threshold. Then, a cry. A cry that wasn't Cait's. I tried to look up, but saw only the outline of a person hovering above me, the shapes made blurry by my damaged eyes.

"Aster?"

I opened my mouth to speak, to agree.

*Yes.*

My brain called the words, but my voice stayed silent.

The person kneeled over me, her shocked face coming into sharper focus as it got closer.

I stared into the eyes of my Grandmother, warm and full of concern, as the world around me dimmed to black.

# CHAPTER TWO

I woke in the guest room where I had stayed when I had first come to the farm. The mattress was still as lumpy beneath me as it had been the last time I had been here, the wallpaper still ancient, slowly peeling away from the walls of the old farmhouse where my dad was raised. If I hadn't known better, I might have been tempted to believe that it had all been a dream. That everything I had experienced in the Fold had been nothing more than a horrible nightmare.

But the skin on my arms, tight and still stinging from where the rain had coated it, would not allow me to deny reality. I shifted a little and groaned as I felt it crack like brittle paper.

Grandma appeared in the doorway, a small bowl in her hands.

"You're awake," she said. "Thank God."

She walked over to the bed and sat down carefully on the edge of the mattress.

"Where's Cait?" I asked, unable to raise my voice louder than a whisper.

"Who, the girl?" she asked. "She's downstairs watching television."

Television. I wondered how she was reacting to something so

unusual.

"Is she okay?"

She took a piece of cloth, dipped it into the solution in the bowl and began patting my wounded arm.

"She'll be fine," she said. "She only got the burns on her hands, and one little spot on her face."

I sighed with relief. The blanket Kiron had gifted to me had proven more magical than I ever would have thought. It must have protected her from the rain.

Her hand paused, and through my blurry vision I saw her glaring down at me. "What were you thinking?"

I ignored her question, still too caught up in my own thoughts.

"Where's Mom?"

"She'll get here in a day or two," she said, resuming the treatment of my arm. A light tingling sensation came to the surface of the skin where she patted. "I called her after I got you up here. You were delirious. If it wasn't for the girl, Cait you call her? If it wasn't for her help, I don't know how I would have done it."

I tilted my head back against the musty pillow and, for the first time in a long time, let myself relax.

Everything was going to be okay now. Cait wasn't badly injured. Mom was on her way. I was warm and comfortable, as comfortable as I could be with my wounds.

Grandma stayed silent for a time, carefully treating every inch of my exposed skin. Both arms, my face and neck, and halfway up my legs were affected and burning. As she spread the liquid over my skin, the pain gradually eased. She handed me the wet cloth.

"Squeeze a couple drops into your eyes," she said. I did as I was told.

The relief was immediate, and slowly the room, and her face, came into clearer focus. I handed the cloth back to her.

Finally, when she had checked me over for any spots she had missed, she set the bowl on the night stand, sighing heavily.

"I don't know how your mom is gonna react, seeing you after all this time," she said.

How she would react? I didn't understand her concern.

"Her heart broke in two when you left," she went on. "I thought I might lose her there for a time. Losing Jack was bad enough, but Dana, too…"

Her voice drifted off, and a thin tear streaked down her cheek.

"I didn't leave," I croaked. I suddenly felt unsure, nervous about the mess I had left behind. "I was, well, I was taken."

Her eyebrows raised high on her forehead.

"Taken? What do you mean? I thought—we both thought that you left. That you were angry about the summer."

I laughed a little, but the effort hurt my insides, and I stopped abruptly.

"I didn't leave on purpose," I said, stifling a cough. "Trust me."

"Well, where did you go, then? Someone took you?" she asked. She looked confused. I guess she had never considered anything other than abandonment as a reason for my disappearance. So few people lived out this way, I could see why kidnapping had never entered her mind. But I hadn't expected them to think I had run off, and a cold feeling of dread hardened in the pit of my stomach. Was this what my mother thought, too? That I had left her? Like my father had?

"Nobody took me," I said. "Not exactly. You remember when I was spending all that time up in the attic? I found something. It was a sort of map, only it wasn't. It was a portal. I've been on another planet, on a few planets, actually, all this time."

I cringed, waiting for her reaction. Now that I was finally speaking the words, the explanation about where I had vanished to, I was terrified. Would she think I'd gone crazy?

Then, she did something unexpected. She smiled.

"I think you've been remembering your Pa's old stories," she said. Her look shifted to pity. "You poor thing. You must be awfully traumatized."

"Dad's old stories?" I asked. My dad had never so much as read me a picture book, let alone told me stories as fantastical as what I had experienced. "No. I'm telling you the truth. I know it's hard to believe."

"Child," she interrupted, patting my hand with her warm, wrinkled palm. "I think whatever you've been through has—"

"That's not it," I protested. "Ask Cait. She'll tell you the truth. I rescued her from the Coyle. She was under his enchantment. And I brought us back here. Grandma, we've been on the other side of the universe this whole time. We've been in the Maylin Fold."

At this, her patting stopped. She stared at me, mouth slightly open, as if I had said the last thing she had ever expected to hear.

"What did you say?" she asked. She looked weirdly terrified.

"I said we've been in the Fold all this time. I met a wizard. His name was Almara. And he had left a map, I think it was originally supposed to be for Brendan, to follow him. Only Brendan couldn't get back to Aeso from here. I was able to, though. Probably because Earth is closer now than it was back then, and—"

"That's enough," she said sharply, standing up from the bed. "I didn't realize your father knew so much about the nonsense passed down the

Wood line. I'm only sorry he told it to you at all."

"Wait. Dad knows about this?" I asked.

"Oh, sure," she said. "Jack knows all the crazy stories from his pa's ancestors. I told Charles years ago to stop telling the stories to him. He was just a child, and fairy tales told as truths help no one. Especially someone with Jack's...problems." She stopped, averted her gaze, and I could tell she was reliving some of her own nightmares. The nightmare of having a sick child and not being able to help him, for instance. "We all have to live in *this* world, no matter how broken it is now."

I was reeling. My dad, all this time, must have known exactly where I was. Or at least he might have had a good idea. Had anyone thought to ask him? I struggled to sit up in the bed, but the skin on my arms gave way, cracking in earnest. I felt the tickling sensation of blood as it trickled down my battered forearms to the bedsheets. I gasped at the pain of it, and soon I was struggling to hold back another coughing fit.

I held out a hand to her, a gesture asking her to wait, to not leave me here alone with so many thoughts swirling in my brain. I had too many unanswered questions.

Suddenly, I felt that I had to find him, my dad. I had to tell him. About these past months. About how I had been healed. Maybe Grandma was wrong. Maybe, all these years, what everyone else had taken for madness had simply been the truth.

And no one had ever believed him.

Was it possible?

"I'm telling the truth," I said, finally catching my breath, my tone nearly begging. "Ask Cait."

"The girl won't talk," she said, her voice as stern as I'd ever heard it. "I don't know where she came from, but she needs to go back home. You can't just pick up kids when you're off having an adventure."

I laughed. I couldn't help myself. She thought I had been out on an adventure? For the fun of it? She folded her arms, not understanding that to take Cait home would require a lot more than just a drive down the road.

Her face darkened.

"I want to know where you've been," she said, walking towards the door. "And trust me, your ma's not gonna be too keen on hearing this nonsense, either."

"Grandma, wait," I called.

But she didn't wait. She strode from the room, her anger overcoming her. And I was left with my mouth hanging wide, lost for an explanation she would accept.

I watched the sky outside slowly darken as the sun set behind the thick blanket of clouds. Overhead, the steady drum of rain gradually lightened until only an occasional pattering could be heard sounding against the metal roof of the farmhouse.

Somewhere out there my mother was driving, on her way here. I imagined her face, set with the determined look of hers I knew so well, like a steel mask shining with her intentions. And what could I expect when she arrived? Would she get angry like Grandma had when I told her the truth about where I had been? I knew the answer to that already.

*Yes.*

For the first time since I had left Earth, I felt something other than longing to see my mother again. The familiar feeling of dread that came with silly things like lost homework and late arrivals filled me. I pushed the feeling down, determined myself to stay strong. She might be angry when she got here. That was fine. I would have to deal with that. But in the end I would have to make her see the truth, one way or another.

Grandma had kept Cait away from me for the entire day. Maybe she was down there trying to get her to talk, to tell her what she wanted to hear. But I couldn't see how some horrible tale of kidnap would be any better than the true story I had told.

Still, part of me understood her doubt. It *was* crazy. Would I have believed some kid from school if they'd come back after a long absence, spouting tales of wizards and monsters and jumping from planet to planet like some sort of cosmic ping pong ball? No, of course not.

Would I have believed it if the person had been Grandma?

I didn't know.

I grew restless lying in the bed. So many days of living on the run had resulted in changing my body from that of a soft, weak-limbed, sick kid to the hardened, lean muscled machine of an athlete. Despite my injuries, I was anxious to be up and moving again.

I looked down at my arms. The cracks had scabbed over, and the skin surrounding them felt noticeably softer than it had before Grandma's treatment. Whatever she had put on my skin had helped immensely. It still felt tight and uncomfortable all over, but my skin had stopped cracking with my movements. I should have stayed in bed for much longer, given what I'd been through. A few days of rest would have done me good. But I needed to see Cait, to make sure she really was alright. Her wounds were probably in the same state as my own by now, irritating, but already on the mend. But I was concerned about what Grandma had said about her not talking. I had promised to take care of her, and I needed her to understand that she was safe here, even if our stories were not going to be believed. Each pang of stinging from my own body reminded me that I was not off to a very good start of presenting Earth as somewhere friendly for her to hide out.

I hobbled over to the dresser and found that Grandma had left an old pair of flannel pajamas for me. The fabric was soft and warm, so unlike the clothes I had been wearing for the past eight months. Putting them on, I was amazed at how easy everything was here compared to in the Fold. Even though Earth was in a steep state of decline, I was warm, fed, and comfortable. It seemed impossibly decadent compared to trekking through the prickly forests of Aeso, or the cold, hard caverns in the Fire Mountains.

I looked out over the fields, long unplowed and unplanted.

*Comfortable but dead.*

These pajamas were from a different time, a time before Earth's deterioration, saved and tended for generations. The green outside had shriveled long ago, leaving only the soil's fruitless attempts to grow the grass anew as it was battered, time and again, by the poisoned rains. Everything in this part of the country had been abandoned decades ago as the people moved into the cities, hiding from the elements. Earth had been built into a place that worshipped excess while it still had resources to waste. Now, all we were left with was what remained from the days when the fields grew green. In time, even these soft pajamas would become coarse and worn. What would remain of our comfortable civilization in a hundred years? Two hundred?

We would lose our comfort as the goods of our ancestors slowly decayed. But we would have no breathtaking vistas to warm our hearts in the place of the lost softness. Only the dead soil would greet our hungry eyes when we went searching for beauty.

The floorboards creaked beneath my bare feet as I moved into the hallway, clutching onto the dark walls for support. As I approached the stairs, my way became easier, lit by the dim electric lights filtering up from downstairs. Sounds of cartoons drifted up the stairwell, and the smell of dinner made my stomach grumble loudly. I couldn't remember the last time I had sat at a table and had a proper meal.

I made my way down the staircase, eager to find the source of the smell. The television came into view, and before it sat Cait. She sat up on her knees, her face just a few inches from the screen. I looked around the room, but she was alone. I walked to the set and knelt down beside her. She glanced at me, then back to the images on the screen, completely entranced.

"Aster," she said, her voice barely above a whisper. "Have you seen this?" Her mouth hung open, as if she had intended to say more, but then, distracted, had forgotten whatever it was.

I sat down heavily onto the floor and put one arm over her chest, pushing her back a little.

"Don't sit so close," I said, parroting the warning I and every other kid on Earth had probably heard a hundred times. "It's not good for your eyes."

She obliged, but only scooted back a few inches. Now that she had found this magical box, where stories and music and entertainment flowed, she seemed unwilling to part any farther away from it than that.

I watched the show over her shoulder. It was a silly cartoon about a rabbit and a fox. Together, the penciled characters danced in a lush, green meadow, singing a song I hadn't heard before.

"It's called television," I explained.

She glanced over.

"What is it?" she asked. "That woman, she doesn't seem to care about it at all. Rhainn-y won't believe this when I tell him. We've *never* seen magic like this." Her eyes were wide, as if she couldn't understand how anybody who possessed such a treasure would ever stray so far away from it as Grandma had.

I smiled, almost laughed. But then I remembered my promise to her, that I wouldn't laugh at her again.

"It's sort of normal on Earth," I explained. "Most people have TVs— er—televisions. We call them TVs for short." Her gaze drifted back to the set, drawn by the howling cry of one of the characters on the screen. "It's not magic. Anybody can get one."

"Can I take one home?" she asked, eyes glued again to the fox, who was now running through the field, his rear-end on fire.

"I don't think it would work at home," I said, leaning back against the wood floor.

It was sweet, watching Cait. Looking around the room, sparse as it was, I realized it was full of things she wouldn't yet understand. Normal things like light bulbs and radios, would seem magical, impossible, to her.

Grandma came through the kitchen doorway and stopped, watching the two of us sitting in front of the television. She looked conflicted. One second, she seemed happy to see us there, safe in her house. Then the next, a cloud came over her features.

"Oh, is the little miss talking now?" she asked, busying herself as she noticed my gaze. She had an armful of salad greens, still black with the gritty soil she grew them in beneath a canopy to protect them from the rains.

Cait looked up at the reproach.

"Sorry, ma'am," she said, her voice small and quiet.

Grandma's face broke into a smile, obviously surprised by the comment from her. She moved across the room to us, wiping her dirty hands on her flowered apron. She knelt down before Cait.

"I don't bite, you know," she said, reaching out one hand and brushing a strand of Cait's brown hair away from her face. "I tried to tell you that before."

Cait didn't recoil, but she didn't lean in, either. I could tell she was uncomfortable.

"Cait can be shy," I said.

Any five year old would be, having lost her family and winding up on a strange, hostile planet.

"You don't need to be shy with me," Grandma said, smiling. "I just want to help you get back to…wherever you came from. Back home."

Cait's eyes grew wide, and she pushed herself away from Grandma, her cartoons forgotten. She leaned up against me like a pup against its mother.

I didn't want to fight. I didn't want to have the same argument again, not when we were just getting settled. But I understood Cait. And I wanted a respite, myself. I needed a break from Corentin rule, just as she did.

I wrapped my arms around her and found she was shaking.

"It's okay," I said. "Nobody is going to make you go back there."

Grandma looked surprised and withdrew her hand, not wanting to scare the little girl further. Her face was confused, concerned, and sad all at the same time. After a few long, awkward moments, she spoke again.

"How about we eat dinner," she said, forcing a smile. "You must be hungry."

Cait peeked out from where she was burying her face in my chest. The kitchen did smell good.

Grandma and I both stood up, and I offered a hand to Cait.

"Don't worry," I said.

Tentatively, she reached out and took it.

Grandma turned off the set and we settled down at the table. She produced a giant bowl of pasta covered in a chunky sauce and handed the serving spoons to me while she tore at the lettuce for the salad. I scooped up a serving of spaghetti and plunked it inexpertly onto Cait's plate. She stared at it, unsure, as I served myself and Grandma.

My stomach was doing backflips as I sat and stuffed the first delicious forkful into my mouth. My tastebuds exploded as I inhaled bite after bite. It wasn't until my plate was half empty that I even looked up to find that Cait had yet to pick up her fork. I hastily wiped my face with one of Grandma's old fashioned napkins.

"You should try it," I said. "It's really good." And it was. Meals served in the Fold, while sustaining, always seemed to be lacking in flavor. My pleasure synapses were firing like mad as I took a piece of buttered bread from a plate nearby and shoved half of it in my mouth.

"What is it?" she asked, wrinkling her nose distrustfully.

"It's called spaghetti," I said.

"Why is it bloody?" she asked.

Grandma laughed, staring back and forth between us uncomfortably, unsure if Cait was joking.

"It's tomato," I explained. "It's a kind of vegetable, only it's got all kinds of spices in it to make it taste really good." She looked up at me, still unconvinced.

I shrugged.

"Suit yourself," I said. "But it's dinner."

She picked up her fork and stabbed at the pasta. Then, when she finally seemed determined to at least try a bite, she lifted the fork up off the plate, only to watch the slippery noodles slide right back off.

"Here, let me show you," I said, leaning over. I took her fork and twirled it around in the noodles until I had a kid-sized bite wrapped around it. "Here."

She took the fork from me and took the first tentative bite.

Her eyes grew round again, but this time from surprise, as she tasted Earth food for the first time. After that, she didn't speak for several long minutes as she mastered twirling bite after bite onto her fork and navigating it into her mouth.

I sat back, my own plate cleared, and watched her, satisfied that I had brought her some joy. For a moment I forgot the turmoil of my return, the sting of my skin. I just sat there, enjoying the sight of this one little girl in the midst of discovery.

I looked over at Grandma and noticed that her own food had been left untouched. She caught my eye.

"How is it that she doesn't know what spaghetti is?" she asked. "Or tomatoes?"

I didn't respond, just stared back at her. She didn't want to hear the answers I had to her questions.

A long silence hung heavily between us. I, unwilling to budge in my account of what had happened to me. And Grandma, who seemed to be trying to decide what to believe.

*She hasn't decided yet. Not for sure.*

"You know," she finally began, "I saw your dad not long ago. There was something about him that rattled me." Her body gave a visible shudder at the memory.

But before she could continue her story, a gravelly sound made us all freeze. It had been so long since I had heard a sound like that, of automation, of technology, that it took me a minute to figure out what it was I was hearing.

Then, it hit me. The sound was of a car crunching down the gravel road as it approached the house. I jumped up from my seat, not bothering to wait for either of them to join me, and headed towards the front door.

# CHAPTER THREE

*Mom.*

She was already crying by the time she was out of the car, forgetting to close the door as she leapt from the driver's seat and ran towards me. My worry about what she would think about my story vanished as I ran for her, and tears pricked at the corners of my eyes, blurring her dark shape. We hit, and I instantly felt that we were two people hanging onto each other for dear life. I pressed my cheek into her lumpy sweater, smelled the laundry detergent, hid inside her arms.

It had always been like this. Just me and her.

She was talking, screaming I think, but I could barely hear a thing as she gripped me to her. After a minute the sound stopped and her crying returned. I pulled away a little, meaning only to look up into her face, but she held me fast. I breathed deeply.

"Mom," I said. "Let go."

"No," she said. "I'm never letting you go again."

Something between a laugh and a cry escaped my throat, and I stopped struggling. All those months I had been out there on my own, waiting for this moment, and now we were here, together.

But, unlike I had expected, the fear that had grown inside me as I had faced down demon after demon in the Fold did not evaporate with the feeling of her embrace. I had thought I'd feel safer, that she would be able to fix everything once I got to her in an instant, her magic more powerful than any wizard I ever could have dreamed up. But nothing changed in that moment except that I was no longer alone. Maybe it was facing reality, maybe it was me growing up a little bit, but I didn't feel any safer than before. Now, reunited with the people I loved, I suddenly had even more to lose. And I was acutely aware that, even though I was home, it wouldn't be for long.

"I thought you were dead," she sobbed into my hair. "I thought—your heart—"

"No," I said, my voice cracking. "My heart's good, Mom."

Somewhere behind me little footsteps tramped along in the dirt, and soon I felt myself being gripped by another pair of arms.

"Don't leave me like that!" Cait yelled, hugging tight to one of my legs.

"I didn't leave you," I said, looking down at the top of her head. "I just came out to—"

"You said you wouldn't leave me alone!" she cried. The temporary joy brought on by her plate of strange spaghetti was gone, and she had fallen back to being terrified.

Finally, I broke Mom's grasp. I only allowed one quick glance into her eyes before I knelt down before Cait.

"It's okay," I cooed, wrapping her in a tight hug. I picked her up and turned to Mom. "This is my mom. Mom, this is Cait."

Mom stepped back, surprised.

"Hello," she said, confused. Then, trying to sound friendly, "Who might you be?" She wiped her face with the palm of her hand and forced a smile.

Cait just glared.

"Aster's mine," she said, wrapping her arms around my neck as if I were her favorite doll.

I laughed.

But Mom couldn't be bothered to be distracted by the cute little girl for long.

"Where on Earth have you been?" she asked me, new tears springing to her eyes. "We searched everywhere for you. We had the police all the way out here. I even went up to that camp you were talking so much about, thinking that somehow you'd made your way there after I told you you couldn't go. But when you weren't there, I—I—"

"I didn't run away," I said, hoping she would believe me. "Mom, it's not like that. It's not your fault."

Tears streamed down her face again, lit only by the dim bulb on the porch Grandma had flicked on.

"And your father," she continued, barely listening. "I found him, out in his shack on the mountain, thinking he had come and taken you. But all he could do was blather on about other planets and aliens and magic and…oh, Aster. Where have you been?"

I froze, my mouth already open to answer her questions, but no words came out.

My father was talking about planets? And aliens? And magic?

Overhead a crack of thunder boomed across the clouds, lightning flashing across the night sky like a fireworks show.

"Better get back inside," Grandma called from the porch. "Last think you need is another burn."

Cait jumped down from my arms, so fast I was almost insulted by how easily she gave me up at the mere mention of the rain. But I couldn't blame her. Even mild injuries could seem like the end of the world to a little kid.

"Another burn?" Mom asked, grabbing my arm and trying to inspect it in the dark. I sucked air through my teeth at her grasp on my still-sore skin.

"Let's go inside," I said, turning, cradling my arm.

"Oh, no," she said. "You're hurt."

I moved towards the house and she followed, wrapping her arms around my shoulders as we walked. It wasn't until we were in the light of the kitchen that she saw the damage that had been done to my body. She let out a little shriek as she took in the red, scaly covering that had been healthy skin only this morning.

"What happened?" she asked, shepherding me over to a chair and practically shoving me down into it.

But my mind was latched onto something else, was racing madly. Dad. He knew what was going on, might have known this whole time.

"We got caught in the rain," I said, distracted. "It's nothing. I'm alright. What did Dad tell you?"

"What do you mean what did he tell me?" she asked, grimacing. *"Where have you been?"*

Cait sat back down at the table, staring back and forth between her half-eaten plate of food and the rest of us.

"He's been with me," she said, picking up her fork and twirling a bite of spaghetti onto it. "On Aeso." She looked up at me and smiled. One of her baby teeth stuck out at an odd angle, and I realized it must be wiggly. "He glows." Then she focused her full attention back on her meal, slurping up her noodles.

I cocked my head. *Glows?*

"Aeso?" Mom asked. "What's that?"

My wonder at Cait vanished in an instant, and I stared back at Mom. I wanted desperately for her to believe me, but I was terrified that she wouldn't.

"Mom, I promise I'll tell you everything," I said. "But first, tell me what Dad said. It's important."

She stared, clearly not understanding why I suddenly had so much interest in the father who had abandoned me so many years ago. Finally, she relented. "Nothing," she said, sitting heavily into a chair across from me. She held her hand out across the table and I put mine into it. She didn't seem to want to let go of me.

Grandma crossed to the kitchen and pulled down a bottle of an amber covered liquid from the shelf.

"It was more of his usual blather," Mom said. "I thought he had been taking his medications, but apparently not."

"But what did he *say?*"

"What does it matter?" she sighed. Then, seeing that I wasn't giving up, continued. "He kept going on about some warrior person on another planet, and that aliens were coming here to invade. It was the same stuff he always used to talk about, only worse. You know he's always been on about other women he's engaged to marry, other planets he's planning to travel to, other *dimensions* he's visited, the voices in his head..." She took the drink from Grandma's outstretched hand and absently set the glass on the vinyl tablecloth, her face disgusted at the conversation. Her fingers worked around the edge of the rim absently. "He didn't look good. He hasn't been taking care of himself. He kept talking about hiding gold."

I reached out, steadying her hand on the glass.

*"He told you he's hiding gold?"* I asked. My heart was suddenly thudding in my chest, and fear started to prickle along the edges of my brain.

"Yes, something about his birthright. It was hard to understand him, Aster. He wouldn't stop. When I tried to get him to sit and talk calmly, to tell him you were missing, it only made him crazier."

"What did he do?" I asked. "When you told him?"

She sat back, eyeballing me.

"He started pacing, as usual," she said. "He didn't speak to me again after that. He just paced around and around. After that, he came back here."

"He came here?"

Grandma slurped loudly from her own glass at the far end of the table.

"That's what I was about to tell you," she said.

"When?" I asked, turning away from Mom. "What did he do? Why did he come?" The brief feeling of comfort I had felt was draining away. What did he know?

"Didn't even barely look at me," she said. Her eyes were wide again, terrified for reasons I couldn't understand. Her own glass was empty now before her, her hands wrapped protectively around it. "He just blew right by me, straight up to the attic. He banged around in there for a good hour, but when I tried to talk to him he just ignored me. Then, just before he left, he came back downstairs. He sounded so normal." Her voice cracked at the memory. "I hadn't heard him speak so clearly since he was your age, since before the illness took him." She stood up from the table and moved to the foot of the stairs, looking up as if she could see the ghost of him descending from the attic as she spoke. "It was right here. He looked me in the eye, told me everything would be alright now. But his eyes—" she broke off, a sob choking her words.

I stood up from the table and approached her, forced her to look at me.

"What about his eyes?" I asked.

"They were—they were—black," she said, her voice barely a whisper. "Like the darkest storm cloud you've ever seen."

Her shoulders shook, with either fear or sobs, I couldn't tell. I stepped back, reeling, and braced myself against the couch.

It wasn't possible. The Corentin's power couldn't reach all the way to Earth from the Triaden.

Or could it? Who was to say he couldn't possess a single soul that walked the barren wasteland that remained?

With a wrench in my gut I remembered Jade's eyes the last time I had seen her, mad from Corentin possession. Black as coal.

And suddenly the completeness of the Corentin's efforts to stop me finding the gold I needed settled upon my shoulders, weighing me to the floor like a stone.

*No. No. No.*

I took the stairs two at a time, not caring when the effort made my skin crack again.

"What are you doing?" Mom called from downstairs. As I gripped the string hanging down from the attic door, I heard her footsteps on the stairway. "Aster, get back here! I'm not done talking to you."

But I couldn't wait. I couldn't delay. I had to know, had to see for myself.

I wrenched the door open, and as I pulled it down, a ladder unfolded. I hauled myself up the rungs, and just as I stuck my head inside the musty space, I felt Mom's hand grip my ankle.

"Where do you think you're going?" she demanded.

I shook my foot free and continued up into the attic.

"He took the gold," I said, breathless. "Oh, God. What are we gonna do?"

"What? What do you need gold for?" she asked, climbing up behind me.

I ignored her. I found the single light and flicked it on. The space looked just like I had left it half a year ago, piled high with boxes and books. Without waiting to explain, I dove in, madly searching through every open box, trying to remember what the one I was seeking looked like. Around me, books and clothes and old trinkets flew as I scoured the place for the one little box that held the key to balancing the Fold, to getting my life back, to saving all the people I had left behind in the Triaden.

In the darkness, my hands closed around it, the old, wooden jewelry box. I was panting as if I had run halfway across Aria. I slid down to the ground and held it in my lap, hoping that it was just as I had left it the last time I had been in this room.

I opened the lid and slipped my hand inside, searching for the familiar snarl of jewelry, the long forgotten treasure gathered hundreds of years ago by my own ancestor for the very same purpose I wanted it for now.

To balance the Fold. To reinsert the gold, so rare and precious in the Fold, into the core of the misaligned planets. To foil the Corentin's plans before he could take the any farther.

I willed it to be there. I prayed for it to be there. I begged the universe above to let it be there.

But the box was empty.

Mom was crying again. I hadn't noticed her enter the attic. She sat down beside me, wiping her tears on the back of her sleeve.

"Baby, what is going on with you?" she asked, overwhelmed. "You're scaring me. Please tell me. Tell me where you've been all this time."

My fingers were still searching every inch of the empty box. Could it be hidden somewhere inside? Maybe there was a secret compartment. But in my heart I knew the truth. He had come for the gold, taken it. Why, I couldn't imagine. But it was gone. I turned to Mom.

"What Dad told you is true," I said. "About the warrior. A champion, they call him. Me, actually." I caught her eye, tried to get her to understand, to believe me. "I didn't run away, Mom. And nobody took me, either. I've been on another planet this whole time, trapped there. A lot has happened, and I will have to go back eventually. I came back here, back to Earth, to get the gold hidden in this box. It was left here by my great, great grandfather Brendan two hundred years ago. Left here for me." I looked down at the empty box. "We have to find Dad."

It sounded insane. I knew it did. But it was still the truth.

"I know it sounds crazy," I said. "But Cait will tell you the same." I imagined Cait's older brother, Rhainn, at the mercy of the Coyle back on Aeso. Remembering his imprisonment slammed a weight over my chest. "We don't have much time. We need to find Dad."

She looked up at me slowly, and I could see in her eyes she didn't believe me.

"It's just the same," she said, shaking her head slowly. "It's just like

Jack. You've gone crazy."

My heart fell. I shook my head.

"He was never crazy," I said, the truth of my own words sinking in as I spoke them. "Not really."

She turned away, leaned her head down into her palms. I put one arm around her shoulders, but she shrugged it away.

I sat there with her for a time, tried to figure out the right thing to say. The only words that would have comforted her were lies, and I didn't have it in me to deceive her into doing what needed to be done. Her crying slowly faded, and she wrapped me in her arms again, slowly rocked me the tiniest bit, as if I were still her sick baby boy.

"You have to believe me," I finally said. "I'm not crazy, Mom."

My heart was breaking as I removed myself from her grasp. I had yearned so many days and nights for the feeling of being held by her, for the comfort of knowing that everything would be okay, that she would make it so.

But I found she could not comfort me now. Not until she understood the truth.

I stood up and started to move towards the doorway. I would have to wait until tomorrow to fully search the attic in the light of day. Just in case something had been left behind that I might now understand. Maybe I would find something that would help her understand, too. Something that would help her believe.

When I reached the hole in the floor, before I took the first step down the ladder I turned back.

"Are you coming?" I asked.

She didn't look up. She was acting like her worst nightmare had come true, and for a moment I wondered if she would have rather gotten the news that I had died all those months ago. I could imagine the future she feared for me now, thinking that I had lost my mind just like Dad. Thinking that I would follow him into madness instead of choosing to stay with her.

As I took the first steps down the ladder, I resolved to somehow convince her. I would make her see.

*They'll all believe in the end. When he comes for them.*

But all I could do in that moment was leave her there, not ready to accept the truth, crying into her hands.

# CHAPTER FOUR

I woke to the sounds of cartoons. In the night, someone had spread a woven blanket over me as I slept, and I pulled it up over my head, relishing the familiar smell of the old farmhouse. The sun shone through the windows, bathing me in warm light, the clouds chased away for the time being.

The night before I had told them the story, the true story, of me finding Almara's map in the attic, of how it had transported me to Kiron's field thousands of light years from here. When I got to the part about Jade getting possessed by the Corentin, the supreme force of evil in all the Fold, Grandma gasped. She kept opening her mouth to speak, and then shutting it again, seemingly thinking better of what it was she wanted to say.

Grandma had gone oddly quiet upon hearing my story again, this time with much more detail than before. And when Mom recounted what Dad had said upon learning of my disappearance, Grandma had retreated within herself. She sat on the cushy armchair that I knew was her favorite, her legs folded beneath her, staring into space in silence.

If one thing had been different about my story of the Fold, it had been in the telling. Nobody could deny that I was calm about it, as calm as I could be, given the circumstances. Unlike Dad, I didn't pace or rant or see things that weren't there. I simply told the events just as they had happened. I simply told the truth.

But in the end, I had fallen asleep next to where Cait had laid, their verdict about my tale still hanging heavily between us all.

I heard the click of the television as someone turned it off, then Cait's scampering footsteps as she ran to me. I peeked out from behind the blanket and saw Mom, looking flustered, as if she had been running around all morning while I slept. Grandma sat across the room at the kitchen table, her hands wrapped around a mug of coffee.

"Up you get," Mom said, grabbing the blanket and pulling it off me in one big sweep.

"Hey!" I argued. "What are you doing?"

Cait climbed onto the couch next to me, either trying to protect me or seeking protection herself, I couldn't tell.

"We're going to the city," Mom said. She plunked my boots down in front of the couch and stood back, crossing her arms.

*So, she's made her decision.*

She didn't believe me.

"Why would we go to the city?" I asked cautiously, sitting up.

"To have you checked out," she said.

"What do you mean, 'checked out'?" I asked.

"Just get your shoes on," she said, turning to Grandma. "Cathy, you coming with us?"

But Grandma didn't respond, only sat there staring just like she had the night before.

"So you don't believe me, then?" I asked. "Is that what this is about?"

Cait, sensing that another argument was in the works, crawled behind me and rested her head on my back.

"You need a doctor," Mom said. "This is just like what Jack did." Her voice cracked, and I could tell she was on the verge of losing it again. "I'm not going to live through that again, Aster. We'll get you settled, get you on the right medications, and then—"

"I'm not crazy, Mom!" I said, trying not to shout. I stood up from the couch, Cait's nervous fingers clawing at my arm. "I'm telling you the truth about what happened. I'm not going anywhere other than to find Dad."

"You listen to me," she said, her voice low. She walked towards me, and I took a step backward at the threat in her tone. "I've been searching this whole damn world for you since you left eight months ago. I'm not going to do that again. I'm not going to lose you again. You still haven't told me where you've been, and that's fine. You can keep your secrets if that's what you really want. But if you think for one second that I'm going to let you go off chasing your father just because whatever he's told you has turned you against me, you're sorely mistaken."

I sighed, rolling my eyes at her.

She grabbed me by the arm and started dragging me from the room.

"Hey!" I said. "Get off!"

I ripped my arm from her grasp and she turned back, surprised. She had never known me as strong, only the weakened boy who had barely ever argued with her.

"I'm perfectly fine, Mom," I said.

Cait ran up behind me, gripping onto my legs. I looked down at her. I needed her backup.

"Cait, what's the funnest thing you and I have ever done together?" I asked.

She looked up at me, her eyes wide and conflicted. Then, when I nodded my reassurance, she spoke.

"Run," she said. "You're super fast." Her face broke into a smile at the memory.

"You hear that?" I asked, turning back to Mom. "I'm healthy now, Mom. My heart is strong. I'm strong. And in the Fold I'm faster than a cheetah."

She made to grip my arm again, but I was too fast for her.

"You are my *son*," she said. Her face was alarmed. Now, her sick kid thought he was as fast as the fastest land mammal on Earth. "You need a doctor, and you're coming with me whether you like it or not."

I flailed as I backed away, trying to avoid her grasp. Cait began to cry, and Mom continued to try to catch hold of me.

"That's enough!"

Instantly, the commotion ceased.

It was Grandma. Nobody had noticed her standing from the table amid the argument, but now she had both hands pressed into the wood and stared at the group of us with a fierceness I had never known she possessed.

"If the boy can run, let him prove it," she said.

Staring at me the whole time, she walked around from the table and towards the sliding back door. Opening it, she stood aside, indicating we should pass.

*She knows something. Something she's not telling us.*

But what?

"Cathy," Mom said, suddenly shocked. "What do you think you're doing? You know Aster can't run."

"I don't know that," Grandma said. "It's been a while since we've seen him try, hasn't it?"

"There's no hospital out here, Cathy," Mom said. "Where will we take him when he collapses?"

But I didn't give her the opportunity to answer that question. I caught Cait's eye and leaned down to whisper.

"I'll be right back. Promise."

Then I broke free from her tiny hands and ran for the door before anyone had a chance to say anything else.

The morning sun felt warm on my healing skin. In the distance, I could hear Mom shouting after me. She was going to be furious with the lot of us, but I didn't care. I knew the truth.

My feet pushed hard into the dirt, already dry and crumbly after yesterday's rain. It felt good to run. I wished I could show them my true speed, the way my feet flew over the ground in the Triaden. But though I was a normal, mortal kid on Earth, my body remembered the tricks it had learned over the past several months, when I had been something more. I told every muscle, ever fiber and cord woven within my burning legs how to move at maximum capacity, just as if I were bounding through the fields behind Kiron's house.

And I flew. As fast as Earth would let me.

I didn't stop until sweat broke out across my face. I turned back, and in the distance all three were specks against the horizon. Echoes of their argument just barely reached my ears, and I smiled. Partly, I was relieved; what I had experienced yesterday had been real. I was no longer sick. Truly.

I took a deep breath and pushed off, back towards the farm. I was in for it, and I knew it, so I pushed harder. If only I could force her to watch, force her to *see* what I had become, then we could stop arguing about details and get down to business. As I made my way closer, I put on a burst of speed, racing towards them, willing them to understand.

Twenty feet away, right on the cusp of what I was feeling more and more certain would be victory, my foot hit a chunk of dirt looser than the rest, and I slipped. I was going so fast that I tumbled, rolling through the remnants of the field, coming to land on my back, squinting my eyes in the bright sun.

Mom shrieked.

I laughed.

She was next to me in seconds.

"Aster!" she shouted, even though she was right beside me. "Are you alright? What were you thinking?"

But I couldn't stop laughing. It felt so good to lose control, to crack up, just like it had felt good to burn my energy running across the field.

Besides, it was funny.

I rolled over, sitting up, and looked at her. I was breathing hard, but evenly, and I grabbed her hand and placed it up against my chest. For a moment her fingers tangled within the fat stone link of Kiron's that hung around my neck. She looked confused, but then her face changed to amazement. She could feel my heart beneath her hand. She could feel my breathing, hard but even. And she could see the smile on my face.

"Do you believe me now?" I asked, finally pushing down the hysterical laughter and meeting her gaze. "I'm healed. How would that ever be possible if I had been here the whole time?" I let go of her hand, and she stared at it, confused. I stood up and walked towards Grandma, who was, for the first time since I had returned, smiling her old, free smile. As I strolled over to her, she opened her arms wide, and I fell into them. I knew I had her convinced.

I turned back and found Mom still sitting in the dirt, staring vacantly at her hand. I started back towards her, and as I did she rose from the ground and faced me.

"It's not possible," she said. "None of this is possible." She looked like she was trying to wake herself from a disturbing dream, one in which it hadn't been determined if it would turn lovely or nightmarish.

I put my own hand over my chest and felt the steady drumming beat of my heart. My fingers brushed up against the link, just as hers had, and I had an idea. Reaching back, I unclasped the necklace and held out the stone.

"I know," I said. "I know it all sounds crazy. Trust me, when I first got there I thought I had lost my mind. But it's real." I walked closer, holding out the stone in front of me. "I'm going to show you something now. Something you really won't believe. But you've got to." I stopped and aimed the link slightly to her left. "Be right back."

My heart thudded, but this time with nerves. Would Kiron's link work here, so far from where it had been created? I spoke the command, and instantly I knew my answer. I felt the world flatten out all around me as I was forced into the jump, tumbling out of it a moment later unknown miles away. I sat on the ground, waiting, giving them a minute to sit up, to realize that I was gone, to ask themselves how I had done it.

*Magic.*

It was the only answer. And once they believed that answer, the rest would follow. It had to.

I stood up, taking in the world around me, now on my own without Cait beside me. How unusual this had all been, returning home. It had been filled with comfort and heartbreak, a bittersweet re-entry into my old life. I did not expect to feel this way.

But excitement was building within me. They would have to believe me now. I raised my arm, pointing the link back in the direction of the house.

When I landed the second time, I found my footing more quickly as I adjusted to the rough magic of the link combined with the forces of this planet. Drawn by the sound of impact, not of my body but of the portal opening on the other end, I heard her screaming as she raced towards me.

"Where are you?" she yelled into the field, searching through the dust to find me.

I walked calmly towards her, emerging from the cloud, hugging her as the force of her body hit mine.

She was crying again.

"Aster, I don't understand," she said, gripping onto me hard.

"It's okay, Mom," I said, patting her on the back. "I told you. I didn't run away." I broke apart from her and held out the link. "I found one of these, a link, in the attic last summer. I didn't mean to do it, but I spoke the command and was transported to the Fold. I've spent the whole time trying to get back here."

She looked between the link and my face, but her confusion was overpowering, and I could tell she couldn't decide if this was real or a dream.

"It really is real," I said.

"It is." Grandma walked slowly towards the two of us. She stopped, putting her hands on our shoulders. She looked happy. Light. Like a kid who was facing something unexpected and wonderful, but who hadn't quite figured out what it was yet.

"You believe me?" I asked her.

She shrugged.

"Didn't want to," she said. "Not at first. Been chewing on it all night. Now this." She paused, looking down at Kiron's link resting in my palm, and I saw that she had tears of her own forming in her eyes. She looked out across the dead fields that had been in our family for generations, now lost to the disintegration of the planet's natural systems. The breeze played with the errant strands of her gray hair, and she smiled. "Let's go back inside. I think we need to talk."

# CHAPTER FIVE

We were back in the attic. All of us. Cait held my hand tightly in hers. After my most recent abandonment, she seemed determined to never let it go again. The floorboards creaked beneath us as we picked our way through the mess. I was happy to see it in the light of day. Whatever drive I had felt to dig through this place before was now tenfold. The mysteries stored up here had been long forgotten by my family, nearly lost forever and protected by the elements by nothing more than a slowly rotting metal roof. Now that I was back, maybe there was more to discover. Maybe now that I knew the Fold, knew my enemy, I would be able to find something of use to bring back with me other than just gold.

We all followed Grandma towards a specific place in the room, the dust brought up by our footsteps dancing in the hazy light. She found what she was looking for and began rummaging through a pile of boxes stacked on the far side of the room. I had never made it this far when I had been searching the attic before, had never seen what was hidden here, and I stopped beside her, curious.

She pulled down a small cardboard box from high up on a shelf. In front of it, a larger box, heavy with books, had hidden it from me before.

She gripped it in both hands and steadied it on the shelf before her.

As she opened it, I realized that, if I had found this box, I wouldn't have bothered with it. Within it were the usual attic discards. Books, a shard of rock, a large saltwater pearl, and what looked like a family album. She quickly found what she was looking for, a small, leather-bound book, and opened it towards the back. Turning to us, she read.

*"October 9, 1879,"* she began.

I gasped.

She went on.

*"My name is Brendan Wood. I came here, a year ago now, from the planet Aria, in search of gold. Using a link crafted by my own hands, I opened the pathway between the planets within the Maylin Fold and Earth, hoping that this place was as rich with ore as legend has told it to be.*

*"Upon entry, I was wounded. Immediately, I tried to forge a new link to take me home, only trying it after several days and at the point I felt certain death was near. It did not work."*

She paused, flipping deeper into the book. Then continued.

*"October 22, 1905*

*"I have tried to pass the knowledge I bring from my ancestors along to my two children, William and Grace. Grace seems to be the most likely to possess magic of her own, and it is with her that I have put in the most effort. Though I fear that now, after many years of believing my tales, she has grown past the age when such things are acceptable within the culture of Earth. Though I have tried to sway them, and also my beloved wife, over the years, there is no magic in this place to prove my own born abilities. What's more, the frame has faded, and it has been many years*

now since I have been able to plot a link at all. I fear the loss of its power is a bad omen for both the people of Earth and the Triaden. Without the ability to travel, the quest of my father, Almara, will be gravely affected. Gold, while not as easy to procure as we originally predicted, I have discovered and saved over the years. Though it is of no use without the means to awaken its power.

"Almara sent me to this place with a link of his own making, a tricky piece of magic meant to guide me back to his location upon my return home. Believing his abilities inferior to my own, I waited some time before attempting to use it to return. By then, I was smitten with the girl who rescued me from the fields I now look out upon. Perhaps my lack of desire to leave her has had an effect on the link's vitality. I know not. What I do know is that, though I have tried Almara's link, year after year, it has yet to show its magic. I fear what this could mean. Perhaps the Earth is yet too far away for the link to work. Perhaps the opposite is true, and the closer it gets to the Triaden the less accurate it becomes.

"But what I am the most concerned about is what the lack of activation on Almara's end could mean. He was meant to work the magic over the link as he went along on his journey, but no life shines from the page when I try to use it to return. Has he died? Has the Triaden fallen to the power of the Corentin? Is there any trail at all to follow? I have no answers."

She flipped through the pages again. Every inch of my skin was prickling with excitement. Never before had I so desperately wanted to read a book.

"October 17, 1924

*"I do not know if the magic has been passed down to my children, but if it has, it does not show itself here. I have done all I can to train them in magical law, but alas with no power to work with, I suspect they have, by now, brushed it off to an old man's musings and forgotten their years of education.*

*"This may be my last entry. Of late, my chest feels heavier than it should, and I find it unlikely that I will last another season. Alas, I have nothing new to report in any case.*

*"I am sealing the last link I have created and leaving it among my possessions for later generations to try. I have spent a lifetime attempting to return to Aria, and with that focus have missed much of the wonders my life here has presented me with. There is no magic here, not of the traditional sort. But I feel something else here that I was missing in the Triaden.*

*"I did not intend for Earth to become my home, and yet it has. Despite all of my attempts over the years to forge a return link back, none of them have ever worked. Now, as I near the end of my life, I have come to peace with the fact that this is where I have come to belong. When I die, I will say farewell to Earth and my family here as though I had been born into this land a son."*

She said the last words softly, then closed the book and handed it to me.

I stared at it, opened it and flipped through it's pages.

It was a *diary*.

*Brendan's* diary.

The television was on again. I had read the diary through twice already, as he had only written once or twice a year during his time on Earth. Now I sat staring at Cait, amazed at how easily she was distracted by the characters on the screen.

Mom now wore the same lost look that Grandma had had all night long. But Grandma was up, busying herself in the kitchen, getting ready to feed us dinner. She seemed renewed, full of energy, with more bounce in her step than I could ever remember seeing her. She was a very old woman, and yet she showed the vigor of someone half her age now. She hummed a song I didn't recognize as she chopped carrots next to the sink.

"We need to talk about our plans," I said. Mom's eyes fluttered as though my words had awakened her.

"Plans?" she asked, looking confused.

"We need to go after Dad," I said. I looked up at Grandma, and she gave me a curt nod.

Now that we were all in a tentative state of agreement, at least about where I had been for the past eight months, I figured it was time to get moving again. Dad had taken the gold. Why, we didn't know. Finding him was our best start along the path to getting our hands on enough gold ourselves to do the job back in the Fold.

"I still don't understand why we need your father for all of this," Mom argued, unwilling to give in completely. "I have a little money saved. Can't we just buy the gold you need?"

The thought hadn't escaped me, but no one in my family had ever had much money. Sure, when the world had still been a healthy and abundant place, the family farm had provided sustenance enough for all of Brendan's descendants that had come after him. But aside from a thin gold band Mom had worn when she and Dad had been married, I had never seen anything of much value. Even that tiny trinket, I think, had been handed down. It had been all we could do to hang on in the cities, hiding from the rain in the giant towers that rose up on every side, fighting to survive just like everyone else. The only other gold I knew of had been here, in this house. And now it was with Dad.

Still, it was a valid question.

"How much gold do you think you could buy with the money you have?" I asked.

Mom looked back and forth between me and Grandma, shrugging.

"I bet that, between the two of us, we could probably afford a couple of necklaces like the ones you saw in the attic," she said. "That's what you were looking for, right? Necklaces?"

I sighed.

"I wanted the necklaces as a starting point," I said, trying to sound gentle. "Even if we find Dad and get back all the jewelry, it won't be enough. We'll need more than that."

"Well, how much then, Aster?" she asked, smacking her hand down on the side table and standing up. "Where do you expect to find all this gold?"

"I haven't figured it all out yet," I said, defensive. "And I need a lot. At least a stone the size of my fist." I held up my hand and clenched it. Then, looking at just how much that was, my heart fell a little.

"Oh, great," Mom said sarcastically. "Well, that should be no problem, then."

"It's not my fault," I argued. "I'm not making this all up, Mom. I'm just following the lore. So no, I don't know where we'll find all that gold. I guess we'll have to be looking for a while, won't we?"

We stared at each other, both heaving with anger. Finally, she turned her back to me and slumped onto the sofa, defeated.

"I think we should leave in the morning," I said to the room.

Originally, I had planned to come back to Earth, grab the gold from the attic, find whatever else I could sell or steal and then return immediately, leaving Cait here in Mom's care until I succeeded in my plans. Or failed. I hadn't expected a journey once here, and now that more and more secrets were coming to the surface, I felt it would be stupid to leave Mom, and especially Grandma, behind.

Under normal circumstances I would have been nervous to see my father. I had never known him, not really, and what memories I had were riddled with frightening events, harsh glances, wild words not meant for a four-year-old boy to hear. Few memories I had of my time with him were good, and I found I often had a hard time remembering him at all.

But now, under the veil of the Corentin's power, a reunion that had once seemed uncomfortable had become a terrifying prospect.

Part of me wanted to see him, needed to desperately.

Most of me wanted to stay far away.

All of me had no choice.

"Mom," I said. "We have to."

"But he's—" She stopped mid-thought, and I could tell she was struggling to reconcile her experience with my father and the reality that now faced her. "He's crazy," she finished, her voice nearly a whisper.

"But he can't be," I argued, not really knowing if I was right or not. My own stomach tightened at the thought of coming face to face with him. All of my experience with the man was the opposite of my proclamation. "We have to remember," I continued, "that this all starts and ends with the Corentin. Everything that has happened on Earth for the past hundred years, the droughts, the crimes, the rains, it's all the Corentin's doing. He thrives on making people suffer, on controlling them."

It was what he was doing to my dad. That was my argument. But it died on my lips. It was too terrifying to imagine now, sitting in comfort in Grandma's living room, that the Corentin's grasp could stretch through the cosmos and reach all the way into the inner workings of my father's mind.

No, not just my father.

Brendan's grandson.

Almara's descendant.

The Corentin's enemy.

"I don't even know where he is," Mom argued. "He could be anywhere by now." It was clear she had no desire to see him again, whether his madness was born to him or caused by an evil force she could barely begin to understand. "Isn't there some other way?"

I sighed.

"It's the gold," I said. "We need the gold, and he took it."

"What do you need gold for?" she asked. "I've never understood why people become obsessed with jewelry and other useless things. You can't eat it. It won't house you. It won't protect you. So why bother?"

"Gold isn't useless," I said. "Not in the Fold. The planets were all knocked out of alignment centuries ago by people stealing the gold that kept them balanced. It's crazy powerful, Mom. A tiny speck of gold is enough to open a portal to the other end of the universe. People raided the inner caverns of the planets, stole it all so that they could travel and do all kinds of magic. They didn't get it."

"But why didn't they just replace what they'd taken?" she asked. "Why not just put it all back the way it had been before?"

"The guy who did most of the damage, Jared, eventually tried to reverse what he had done. But gold is so rare that he was never able to find enough to rebalance the planets. So he set a spell. He drew Earth towards the Fold, thinking he'd be able to get the gold from here and realign everything.

"But then everything went completely haywire. He died from the effort, and once Earth started moving towards the Fold, things started to really fall apart."

I stared across the room, imagining what it must have been like when things first took a turn for the worse. Jared must have been terrified.

"There is no gold there," I went on. "And if we don't find it here and bring it back, things on Earth will get worse and worse until the Corentin has just as much power over us as he does over the people back there."

Cait shifted in her seat. Her eyes were still on the TV, but I wondered if she was listening.

"Who is this Corentin person?" Mom asked.

"Only the most evil person you could ever imagine," I said, almost laughing and then thinking better of it. Cait shifted again. "Trust me, Mom. We all want Earth to stay as far away from him as we can manage."

"But Aster," she said, her eyes focusing again. "Earth is a *planet.* How are we supposed to control an entire planet?"

I stared at her and realized I didn't know the answer. I didn't have the trajectory of how, exactly, to fix every single thing that was wrong. I was just one piece on the board in what was a much larger game.

"I don't know," I finally said. "All I know is that, if we can get the gold, it'll help. It's the whole reason Brendan came here in the first place. There are people back there, wizards, who can help us once we have it."

"I don't understand why it has to be us, though," she argued. "If there are…wizards…or whatever these people are, why can't they handle things? We're just normal people, Aster."

"*You* are," I said, picking at a piece of dried skin on my arm. It was coming off in flakes now. "But I'm a Wood. And so is Dad. It's kind of our duty, I guess."

"I'm already half-packed," Grandma said, bringing a huge bowl of vegetables over to the kitchen table. I hadn't realized she had been listening. "We'll leave in the morning."

"But Cathy," Mom started to argue.

Grandma held up her hand, silencing her.

"Listen to me, Dana," she said. "I've lived most of my life now dealing with the curse of all this hanging over my family. And I know you've had your fair share of it, too, but it's not the same. I sent my son away, nearly sent his father away before him and probably would have if he had lived to today. I heard the stories as they were passed, and I ignored the truth in them. I ignored the history until it became, in my mind, myth. Well, it ain't myth. Not anymore."

She turned back, walking into the kitchen and taking a plate from the oven. She paused with the food in her mitted hands, looking through the window out onto the fields, her fields, stretching as far as the eye could see, dead and withered.

"It's time," she finally said.

She set down the plate on the counter, removed the mitts and brushed her hands across her apron. She untied it from behind her back, slipping it over her head and folding it neatly.

"It's time for me to go get my son."

# CHAPTER SIX

After dinner was over and Cait was asleep, I made my way back up to the attic, bringing a flashlight and another lamp with me. I still had work to do up here, and I didn't know what I was looking for.

I started shuffling through the same box Grandma had gone through. The family album was worn, at least a hundred years old, and I flipped through it, searching for clues. Stoic faces looked back up at me as I saw, for the first time, the man who had set all of this in motion.

In the very front of the album was a picture of Brendan and a woman on what appeared to be their wedding day. Brendan's face was dark, tanned from long hours spent working in the sun, and his skin seemed to shimmer like it was painted with gold. The technology of the day meant they couldn't smile for the photo without blurring it, so they sat perfectly still, their faces slack. But his eyes were bright. Like he couldn't believe it had been his good luck to jump across the universe and find his new wife, the woman sitting beside him.

The book was smattered with images of the farmhouse, in much better repair and before the shingle roof had been replaced with the coated metal sheeting, resilient against the rains. Every ten years or so a newer photo would crop up, dated along the bottom edge of the page, the house surrounded by thick, vibrant fields of corn. Images of Brendan's family became more common as the technology of the age changed, and soon the people smiled for the pictures. In one, which must have been taken around Christmastime, the four of them sat around the dining room table we had just eaten dinner at. Brendan sat with his hand on the table, gently placed over his wife's. The children, nearly grown, smiled up at the camera, clearly excited by the festivities. The last photo in the book was, again, of him and his wife. Brendan's hair had grayed by this time, his face had paled, but he still had that look of vibrance about him, a shine to his skin that hinted at something humming beneath it. I wondered for a moment if my own skin looked like that in photographs, if I had the same hint of power flowing through me.

I closed the book and decided I didn't. I had never seen anything of the sort. Perhaps my blood was too diluted, its power cut in half generation after generation, even though it felt, to me, enormously strong.

I sat back and looked around the cramped space. Something felt different up here, but I couldn't put my finger on what it was. I clicked on my flashlight again and ran it over the boxes stacked along every side of the room. A tiny glint of gold caught my eye, peeking out from between two boxes.

*The map.*

The thought hit me like a truck, and my breath caught in my chest.

The first thing I had ever found up here had been a map. Not Almara's paper map, but a much bigger one, painted in fine detail along the far wall. I had cleared everything away from it that first afternoon, had gazed upon it each time I paused in my digging to take a breath.

But now, someone had covered it up. That was what was different.

I sprang to my feet, grabbing at the boxes and hauling them away from the wall. Behind them, as I slowly revealed the paint, I found the map was unchanged, the same odd shape it had been when I had first looked upon it. I stood back, wiping the sweat from my face, and stared, confused.

Why would someone want to hide the map? And who?

There was only one answer to this question, and my heart thudded as it came to me.

*Dad.*

But why?

I heard a creak and looked over, finding Mom watching me from the opening to the hall.

"Hi," she said when I noticed her. "Can I come in?"

"Yeah," I said, trying not to look too terrified about the discovery I had just made.

She picked her way across the space.

"I'd never been up here before yesterday," she said, looking around. She paused, staring at the wall. "What is that?" she asked.

"Some sort of map," I said.

"Of what?" she asked. "What do those rings mean?"

I stared at the rings, glinting mysteriously in the dim light.

What *did* the rings mean?

In the Triaden, the golden ring on Almara's map always indicated the target, the desired destination. Where was this map of? And what *was* beneath those rings? I walked up to the wall, stretching out one hand and running a finger along the curve of gold paint.

"Have you ever seen a shape like this?" I asked, ignoring her question. "Like the whole map, I mean."

She stood back and regarded the wall, studying the outline.

"I don't know," she said. "It looks sort of like America."

"That's what *I* thought," I said, remembering that first afternoon when I had found the map. "But it's not quite the same. I could never figure it out before. Why does it look all squished?"

Mom stared at it, her head cocking slightly to one side as she examined it. She, like I, was searching for familiar landmarks. Suddenly, she took in her breath sharply.

"Ah!" she said. "You know what this is. It *is* America. Only it's America before it was part of the United States. Or, at least, before it had all the states. Look."

She walked up to the wall and pushed back a row of papers on a shelf on the far left side. Behind them, another, thinner line of gray paint appeared.

"This map was made before most states was part of the country."

"Whoa," I said, my brain jamming with the realization that the map continued farther along the wall. This whole time I had only been viewing part of it.

We both dove in, clearing away every book, every sheet of paper, and then every shelf, until the entire wall was completely exposed. It was undeniably a map of the United States. But when Brendan had painted it, not every state was yet in the union. That was why a darker outline cut down the middle of the bigger map. It was the edge of the country at the time. I had thought it was the outer edge when I had first found it, but the map had continued on. Light gray paint, badly faded, outlined the rest of the territories that weren't yet states. I had never seen it, thinking that the black line running down the center had been the border.

But I wasn't concerned about the details of United States history, because Brendan had painted something much more important than a record of the union. In a line much thicker than the other rings, a band of shining gold was now revealed, all the way towards the corner of the room. Along that edge, in the detailed hand of a cartographer, was California. And right over the corner where it met Nevada, the gold ring shimmered.

"What does it mean?" Mom asked again.

I ran my fingers along this new gold line.

"These are all destinations," I murmured, transfixed. I turned to her, smacking my hand against the ring hovering over California. "We need to go here. This is where Dad is."

I expected her to argue. After it taking so long to convince her of where I had been, it seemed only logical that she would.

But she didn't. She stepped up beside me and together we looked back at the wall.

"When I found him," she said, running her hand along a different gold ring, "he was here." She was pointing to the center of the country. "Right near Denver."

"He must have seen this," I said. "Dad must have figured out the same thing we just did. Mom, I think he's trying to hide from us."

"What do you mean?" she asked.

"This wall used to be exposed, but now it's been covered up. I think that when Dad came up here for the gold, he must have seen this map."

"But why would he hide?" she asked.

I didn't know. I didn't have any idea why he would hide or why he would steal the gold. I had never understood the workings of my father's mind.

"I don't know why," I said. "But he covered this up before he left. He didn't want this map found."

I stared at the spot where her hand still lingered, the spot she had said was near Denver.

"Do you think he's still there?" I asked, a plan forming in my mind.

She shrugged.

"I don't know," she said. "But I'd be willing to bet, if he really has seen this, if he's not in Colorado anymore, he's where one of these other rings are."

I couldn't have agreed more.

An hour later we had both made our own version of the map on paper. It made sense for us to have more than one copy, just in case. Once they were complete, we compared them to an atlas from the 1950's to get our bearings. Next to each penciled ring on our papers, we wrote the names of the closest cities.

Chicago

Denver

Salt Lake City

Sacramento

That was where the biggest ring had been, the spot on the wall where Brendan had made his biggest marks. That was where we needed to go.

As the clock passed midnight, we sat across from each other at the kitchen table. Cait lay snuggled beneath a pile of blankets in the living room.

"I think we should call it a night," Mom said, yawning.

I looked over at the pile of backpacks Grandma had dug out and filled with who-knows-what. This was our last chance before leaving. My last chance to make sure I had all the information I could find.

The map was a huge breakthrough. Even though I felt compelled to stay, to dig around upstairs for another week or three, I knew we had to leave. We were as ready as we were going to be.

I nodded, pushing back from the table. I folded the new, copied map and stuffed it in my back pocket. Then I tucked the photo album under the crook of my arm. If I ever saw Jade again, maybe she would like to see the photographs of the brother she had parted from so many years ago.

It had been decided that we would take the car as far as it would go. Grandma had a store of gasoline in the barn, along with several barrels of purified water, and we rigged an old trailer to the sedan to carry it all in.

"Do you think we'll have enough water?" I asked her. I had already loaded five large containers of it, but it was competing for space in the trailer with the fuel.

"Depends," Grandma said, hauling another jug and fitting it neatly into the remaining space. "How long you think we'll be going for?"

I shrugged. I had no idea what to expect. Days? Weeks?

"Well," she said, looking around the barn, "I have enough to keep things up and running here." A water tank taller than my head sat in one corner of the barn, filled halfway with already purified water. "I've hooked up the dripping system for the vegetables, so they should be good to leave for now. But we can only take so much."

I made sure to take a long drink for the tap before we left.

We would have reached our destination more quickly if we were to jump, and I fumbled with the link, now tied securely back around my neck. I hadn't noticed any difference in its power when I had used it yesterday; it had transplanted me safely back and forth again in my attempt to get Mom to believe my story.

But Brendan's diary entry weighed heavy on my mind. He had specifically written about how the magic in his frame had dissipated over time, and I worried that using the link too much too soon would leave us stranded in the deserts of America before long.

I stuffed it back beneath my shirt, determined to save it for when we had no other choice.

As the last of our bags were loaded into the trunk of the car, I opened the back door, grateful that we would be traveling during the winter months. The burning heat of mid-summer in a car with no air-conditioning would have been difficult to manage with just two travelers. But four, one of them a little kid, would have been miserable.

There was one clear advantage to taking the car, though the link would have been much quicker, and I thought of it as I scratched at my damaged skin. The car would provide us with cover from the rain, better than any tarp of blanket could. If we were to become stuck out in the elements with no shelter, it would only be a matter of time before we each succumbed to an extremely painful death. The beat up sedan with its rusted edges would actually protect us quite well, and would allow us to travel *through* the acid rain, not just hide from it.

Mom estimated it would take us a day to reach Denver, which was on the way to California and the last place she had seen Dad. A stir of excitement spun around in my stomach at the thought. Not far from Denver was the camp I had so wanted to visit, the camp for sick kids. Though it seemed silly now, the idea that a place existed somewhere up above the reach of the poisoned atmosphere, where people could pretend things were just as healthy as they had been before the drought, was thrilling. The steady beat of my heart beneath my shirt meant that I might not fit in in a place like that anymore, but after just a few days back on this barren planet I was eager to see some green.

Denver was widely known to be all but abandoned, and I hoped we wouldn't be there for long. It sat at the sweet spot in elevation where most of the pollution that plagued Earth's survivors collected. Above it, the air was clear, the rain was clean. But within it… I clutched absently at my throat as I imagined breathing in the chemicals that were so strong they fused with the clouds, corrupting the rain.

We would not be able to stay there for long.

Cait came around the side of the car, then stood back, staring at it distrustfully.

"What is it?" she asked.

I cranked down my window behind the driver's seat to talk to her.

"It's called a car," I said. "It can take you from place to place."

"You don't have horses?" she asked, not convinced.

"No, not anymore," I said. "Don't worry, though. This is even safer than horses. And more comfortable, too." I reached over to her side of the car and opened the door, indicating that she should come around.

She climbed up into the seat, and a flicker of excitement flashed across her face. Her hands moved over everything she saw, materials she had probably never imagined before.

"So, it's like a horse?" she asked, fumbling with the window crank on her side.

"Here," I said, reaching over and showing her how to lower the window. "And no, it's nothing like a horse. But it will get us to where we're going."

I watched her for a moment, her eyes bright the discovery of this new, unexpected technology. I wondered what else those little eyes saw.

"Hey Cait," I said. "Yesterday you said something about me glowing. What did you mean?"

She paused, her fingers still on the crank, and turned.

"Well," she began, her face scrunching as she searched for the words. "I can see the glow in people. Mama says it's my gift."

"Oh," I said. "Does everybody glow?"

"No," she said, her attention drawn back to the operation of the window. "But you do." Her eyes grew distant, as if she were tracking something far away. Her little hand raised up and made a swirly sort of motion in the air, as if she were drawing a picture.

Mom opened the driver's side door and climbed in, ending our conversation. She leaned over and started the car with a flick of her keys.

"You kids ready?" she asked. We could have been headed out on the first leg of a family vacation from the sound in her voice.

"Yup," I said. "Where's Grandma?"

Mom looked around, spotting Grandma on the covered porch of the house. She was turned towards the front door, fumbling with a key. Mom stepped out of the car.

"Come on, Cathy," she called. "Nobody's going to come through here."

Grandma turned and shuffled towards the car.

"I ain't taking any chances," she huffed as she approached. "There's a lot more in that old place than any of us ever realized. Just wanna make sure it's still there when we get back."

Locking the front door wouldn't be enough to keep people out, and I might have worried about leaving the house abandoned and unprotected if I had seen anyone within a hundred miles of this place in the last five years. But this part of the country was so desolate, so exposed. It seemed possible that no one would ever come this far out again.

She climbed in on her side with a groan, dropping her gigantic purse on the floor beside her feet. It looked like she had packed the entire contents of her bedroom into the old, leather bag, and I couldn't help but question her.

"Grandma, why did you bring your purse?" I asked. I couldn't fathom what she might have stashed inside that would be beneficial to our trip. It wasn't like we were headed to the market.

She turned, not just her head but her whole body, and stared at me.

"You think you're so smart," she teased, "with your little trinkets and your stories. I got a few tricks up my sleeve, too, kiddo."

She shut her door with a snap and Mom reversed away from the house. Then, putting the car into gear, we set off.

Cait stared excitedly out her window as the fenceposts whipped by. I longed to question her more, but somehow I felt that more conversation about such unusual things as glowing humans might be too much for Mom to handle. The old, gravel road was rocky and full of potholes, bouncing the car this way and that as Mom careened down it. She had always preferred to drive fast, and I could relate to her desire for speed, especially considering the situation. But I glanced nervously behind us at the trailer, the fuel in the barrels sloshing back and forth with every bump.

"Careful, Mom," I warned. "The gas is gonna all leak out if you don't slow down."

"Don't tell me how to drive, Aster," she shot back. But in the rearview mirror I saw her glance at the barrels behind us, and the car gradually slowed.

Cait bounced around the back seat, investigating every crevice of her new traveling space. She opened all the little compartments, fingered the couple of coins she found loose in the cup holders, checked in the pocket in front of her seat for hidden treasures in the folds.

But as we turned off the gravel road and onto the slightly smoother highway, her excitement came to a halting end. Her face paled, and with each rocking movement of the car her head swayed back and forth, her eyes rolling back slightly.

"Mom, we need to stop," I said.

"What?" she asked. "Why? We just got started."

"Cait's going to be sick, Mom, stop the car!" I shouted.

Cait's eyes were suddenly bulging, and I turned her head to face the door on her side, pulling desperately on the handle and getting the door open just in time. She vomited all over the pavement. I held her long brown hair away from her face and tried to hold my breath at the same time.

A new knot of worry tightened in my stomach. It had never occurred to me that riding in the car might be a problem.

Mom put the car in park and stepped out.

"Oh, honey," she cooed, coming around the side of the car. "Oh, no, that's not very fun. Cathy, can you pass me a bottle of water?"

She brushed the remaining hair out of Cait's eyes. Cait spit onto the ground repeatedly, her body clearing itself out. When it appeared she was finished, Mom straddled over the sick and put her hands beneath her armpits, hauling her out of the car and into a tight embrace. She walked with her away from the vehicle and, finding a spot on the side of the road, sat down, cradling her in her arms.

My heart suddenly swelled with pride and admiration for my mother. Though her words were inaudible from inside the car, I did make out the comforting murmur she had always used with me in times of trouble. They sat for a few minutes, Mom gently rocking Cait, and soon a giggle escaped the little girl. It was a welcome sound.

The two stood up, Mom taking her hand and leading her around to the other side of the car. I shut the door on the vomit side as Mom opened the door on the other, grateful for the luck that had sent the entire episode of sick landing outside the car instead of on the seat. I scooted over to allow room for Cait, but her smile vanished at the sight of the open car door.

"It'll be okay, hon," Mom encouraged. "Remember what I said. Just look out the window the whole time and take little sips on your water. It'll help. You can talk to the rest of us without looking at us, okay?"

Slowly, Cait nodded, climbing into the seat next to me, immediately training her eyes on the horizon.

Mom slid into the driver's seat again and put the car into gear. Grandma dug through her purse and produced a small plastic bag, passing it back to us.

"If you feel sick again, put it in here, alright?" she asked. I handed the bag to Cait, and she nodded.

The car started moving forward again. I leaned over and cracked her window wider. Immediately her face relaxed, and as the cool breeze fluttered through her hair, a little of her color returned.

"I don't like traveling this way," she said to nobody in particular. "Riding with Aster is much smoother. And faster."

I smiled to myself, then noticed Mom's eyes staring at me, perplexed, in the rearview mirror.

Of course, she would have no way of understanding what Cait meant. To her, it had been at the edges of her ability to grasp that I was healthy at all, that something as awesome as Kiron's link could even exist in the real world. The thought of her ailing son practically flying across the plains seemed too much to ask of her at the moment.

The car drove on, and none of us spoke. Eventually, Cait drifted off to sleep, the plastic bag clutched tightly in her fist.

I stared out the window, watched the dead earth pass us as we rocketed across it.

Grandma had her window down, too, and her fingers drummed lazily against the crack where it disappeared into the door. Her face was serene and calm as she gazed across the land.

Noticing me watching her, she smiled.

"I told you," she said. "I always did want to travel."

# CHAPTER SEVEN

Mom and Grandma drove in shifts. Every couple hours we would stop, stretch our legs, search for signs of the still far-off mountains on the horizon. After a few shift changes, I had an idea.

"Maybe you should let me try driving," I suggested.

Grandma looked at me in the rearview mirror, and Mom turned her head slightly at my voice. Then, together, they both started laughing.

"What?" I asked, defensive.

They didn't answer, and their silence irked me. Sure, I was only thirteen, but I had been through more than any other thirteen year old I'd ever met. If I could fight in battles and lead revolutions, I could figure out how to turn a steering wheel.

But I didn't argue. California was a long way from here. Eventually, they would get sick of driving, and then I'd be the one laughing. Still, I folded my arms tightly across my chest and glared out the window.

The clouds were starting to form, threatening the usual afternoon rain, and I leaned over Cait's sleeping body and rolled up her window.

"How long has it been?" I asked, trying hard not to sound like a little kid. Grandma glanced back again.

"Eight hours," she sighed. "Six to go."

I was bored. I couldn't help it. I would have much rather jumped the whole way than sit in a car for days on end. I pulled out the diary and flipped through it.

*January 12, 1893*

*Six attempts I have made in the past year to make my way home. The linkmaking I do in secret, of course. Josephine would not understand the magic of a frame if she were to see one, though she is no fool. The technology of this place is not yet advanced enough to avoid the fear I'm sure the process would bring her, despite her intelligence and her delicious knack at humor.*

*But each time I make the attempt to use the links I create, I make sure I am near her, her hand in mine. Sometimes I whisper the word, hoping she will be distracted and not think me mad. Sometimes I find other ways to slip it into conversation. Stories are good for disguising my true intentions. I will sit us around our outdoor fire, have the children hold our hands, and at the end of the tale shout the command to the heavens. They find it great fun, and will later traipse around the farm using the words of power from my homeland in their games. It makes my heart sing and hurt at the same time, watching them. I fear that they will never truly know their father if I fail in my attempts to bring them to the Triaden.*

*As time wears on, though, I find myself torn between the duty to my own father and the Fold and that which I feel towards my new, young family. I cannot leave them here if I find a way back. Marcus has died in the last year, leaving me to lead the farm duties on my own. Josephine already has her hands full with the little ones and the many other chores she is forced to undertake, though she makes no complaint.*

*I should not have married. I should have stayed focused on the task set before me, on righting the wrong I, myself, caused.*

*But she is my love.*

*Aside from the logical reasons, I would not leave her under any circumstances I can imagine. And, of course, the children. They grow stronger each day. Grace's babbles have become commands. William's messes have become inventions. Who knows what they might accomplish if given access to a deeper power they do not yet know they possess?*

*I wish I could share this crucial part of my life with Josephine. I wish I could tell her where the father of her children is truly from.*

*So I seek to find a way to reunite the two families I am now part of, and to keep everybody safe in the same motion. When the deed in the Fold is completed, I will let my beloved Josephine lead me where she may. Perhaps she will find the mountains behind Riverstone to be as beautiful as the plains of Earth.*

The rain was pelting the windows now. I closed the book and looked out at the colorless landscape, dark and dangerous with the coming of the rain.

Cait was awake, staring out her window. Her hands gripped the handle on the door, her knuckles white from the tightness of her grasp.

"Hey," I said, tapping her shoulder. "You okay?"

She turned, and I saw that she was not at all okay. She scooted over and huddled up beside me, mashing her face into my chest.

"Hey, it's alright," I soothed, realizing what the problem was. "The rain can't get us inside the car."

"It's so loud," she whimpered.

"I know," I said.

I was tempted to ask her about her own experience with rain, to relate the noise to that she might have heard on her own rooftop back home.

But then I remembered that she no longer had a home to speak of. The last time she had seen it, she had watched her parents die at the hands of the Coyle.

My impatience ticked up a notch as I settled for just holding onto her. The threats we faced here were nothing, I knew, compared to what those back in the Fold were battling. My thoughts drifted to the friends I had left in the Hidden Mountains. Were Kiron and Chapman and all the others still safe?

The rain grew louder, and thunder cracked overhead. Cait jumped, wrapping her tense arms around my middle. I hoped that she would adjust to the journey, that the process of navigating through the mess the Corentin had made of Earth would become easier for her as the days passed by.

But I knew the truth. Facing pure evil, no matter how often you do it and no matter how many different, diluted forms it may take, is never something that becomes easy.


As night fell, Mom turned the car down a wide avenue. Once, stoplights had directed the traffic in this part of the world, but now they hung, swaying slightly in the wind, black.

We were in an old suburban neighborhood, long abandoned by the people who had once lived here. As we passed house after corroded house, I thought of Grandma and her determination to stay out in the country on her own. She really was alone. The people in this town might have found ways to make life work here, like she had in the country, but they had all abandoned their homes when the danger struck. Grandma was one of the very few who had remained in her home anywhere, determined and unwilling to join the masses who had fled to the cities.

It was spooky driving down the road, like tiptoeing through an ancient cemetery. Strangely, I felt more scared in this place than I had in many of the much more dangerous situations I had experienced in the Fold. The place felt haunted, and I searched the dark streets half expecting to find supernatural beings hiding in the shadows made by our car's headlights.

I didn't see a single person, though. Nobody stepped forward to inquire about the strange car coming into the town. But the chills that had started running down my spine didn't stop. The houses reminded me of videos I'd seen of shipwrecks at the bottom of the ocean, the walls eaten away by years of rain, roofs collapsed, untreated metal rain gutters warped and twisted so that it looked like they were slowly melting into the ground.

These had been people's homes. Children had played in these cracked streets, parents had tended their front gardens where now there was only dust.

It was a graveyard.

"There," Grandma said, pointing. "Let's try that one."

She was looking at one of the smaller homes, this one made of brick. Most of the roof was gone, but the walls were in much better shape than the other wooden houses on the street. We pulled into the driveway, the brakes on the sedan squeaking loudly as Mom stopped the car. She flicked off the lights and killed the engine, and we all sat in silence for a few long moments.

Blackness. The rain had stopped, but it was so dark that I couldn't tell if the clouds still hung overhead. When my eyes failed to pick out even a single pinprick of light in the sky above, I decided the clouds had remained.

"Well," Mom said, dropping her hands from the steering wheel, where they had been clenched, "should we go in?"

Nobody answered, but a minute later Grandma opened her door. Mom followed, clicking on a flashlight she had stowed in her car door. Cait hugged me tighter, but I grasped her arms, releasing myself.

"Come on," I said. "It'll be okay. It's just a house."

In the darkness I could just barely see her terrified eyes looking up into mine. I tried to appear brave, in control, as if I believed my own words. I opened my door and stepped out onto the driveway, holding out a hand for Cait, who took it and followed. I reached back in and grabbed my backpack, another gift from Kiron, given under such different circumstances than these that it felt like a lifetime ago. Together, Cait and I followed Mom and Grandma up the stone walk.

The front door was locked, but the windows on either side were broken. Someone had already cleared the sharper glass edges from the one on the right, and Mom slipped one leg through and climbed inside. She came around, unlocking the door, and we all followed her in.

Her flashlight bobbed along the walls as we walked, kicking the pieces of roofing out of our path that had come down over the years. Then, the low ceiling suddenly gave way to sky, and we found ourselves in what remained of the kitchen. Over every surface, chunks of roofing material were scattered. But most of the actual roof was gone, long since rotted to dust by the driving rains. Beneath the film of decades of decay, the once familiar trappings of family life remained. A long, stone countertop ran the length of the space. A refrigerator, one door open, stood empty and partially melted, only the aluminum handle retaining its true original shape.

As we all stood, frozen in what was once somebody's home, the only sound was our tense breathing. Part of me expected someone to come blazing out of the hallway, set to defend their property. But the truth was, nobody was here, which was somehow even worse. Finally, Mom spoke.

"Our best bet is the basement," she said, craning her neck around a corner to look beyond the room. "It'll be the most protected. This roof must have lasted for at least a little while, and the walls would have taken some of the brunt of the weather. I've seen places like this before."

I believed her, but I couldn't remember ever having been inside a home like this. Grandma's farm was built centuries ago, before things like full basements even existed. But if Mom was right, we might get lucky enough to find a dry place to sleep tonight.

She took a few tentative steps out of the kitchen, finding another hallway off to one side. We followed her, and soon found a wide staircase leading down below the house. Once, the stairs had been carpeted, and the stubby, rotten remains of it hung in chunks over the creaking wood.

Down below was left mostly unchanged. The roof above seemed secure enough, and it must have kept most of the rain out all this time. Here, the carpet was thick. A large screen television stood in one corner of the room, bigger than any I had ever seen, with two couches arranged around it. Off to one side, a long, wide table stood prominently displayed.

Mom smiled.

"Cathy, look," she said. "They still have the cues!" She walked to the wall behind the table and taken down a long, wooden stick from a panel where several others were mounted.

"What's a cue?" I asked.

Mom looked at me, the happiness in her eyes faltering for a moment. Then she recovered.

"This is called a pool table," she said, bringing the stick over. She bent down, rummaging in a compartment set deep within the table. A clacking sound echoed from the wood, and when she lifted her hand out she had two round balls in it. She placed them on the table and began searching for more.

Grandma turned, smiling at me and Cait.

"Back in the old days, the snows would come down fierce in this part of the country," she said. "Kids would be stuck inside for days on end sometimes with nothing to do except drive their parents crazy. The farmhouse doesn't have a basement. It was built in the days before such things. We only had a small cellar to hide in when the tornadoes came. But later, people started building these big basements and used them as living spaces for the family. Don't need a tornado cellar when you've got a whole giant room underground."

Mom had produced several of the balls now, each painted a different bright color. Cait was already at the side of the table, one ball in each hand, rolling them back and forth and clacking them together. She smiled.

"So, this is a game?" I asked.

"Yup," Mom said. She was gathering all the balls and placing them within a triangle of wood she had fetched from the wall. Cait and I stood back, watching her intently, while Grandma explored the rest of the room.

Mom removed the wood and took the one ball she hadn't put into the triangle to the other end of the table, placing it onto the fabric surface and then leaning over the table with her stick. Then, with a burst of energy, she flicked the stick, hitting the ball, which rocketed across the table and slammed into the others. They burst out of their formation, clicking against each other and the table edges as they slowly came to rest.

Mom sighed, smiling wide.

"*That* felt good."

Across the room, Grandma slumped into one of the couches and put her feet up. A loud sigh escaped her.

Cait walked over to the wall, grabbing one of the cues and aiming it at the table like Mom had.

"Whoa, whoa, wait a minute," Mom said, placing a hand over the wood. "You have to be careful. You don't want to rip the felt." She propped her own cue up against the table, then went around behind Cait, holding the stick at the same time as her, showing her how to position her body. Then, together, they took a shot. The balls met with a satisfying click, and Cait smiled.

I couldn't resist. I took down a cue as well and the three of us took turns shooting at the balls, though Mom was the only one to get any into the pockets, insisting that was the whole point of the game.

It felt good to play something, to do something that had no other purpose than fun. Eventually, Mom stood back, crossing her arms over her chest as she leaned back against a wall, watching. She had an odd, satisfied look on her face. I hadn't seen her look so relaxed since I had arrived, and it was a relief. It seemed like just seeing her smile was enough to chase away the chills that this abandoned neighborhood had brought me.

Eventually, she yawned and joined Grandma on the couch. But she didn't make us stop playing. They had been driving all day while Cait and I had slept for much of the journey, and she didn't seem to mind the noise. Finally, long after they had both dozed off, I put my cue back up against the wall.

"We should probably go to sleep, too," I said, stretching my arms wide with a groan.

"Just one more," Cait said, sticking out her tongue at an odd angle while she lined up a shot. She took it, and for the first time one of the balls made it into a pocket, though I'm not sure it was the one she was intending. She giggled. "Did you see that?"

I smiled broadly.

"Yup," I said. "Come one." I held out one arm, and she took my hand.

We each took one end of the remaining couch, which was so long that we both had enough room to stretch all the way out with just our toes touching. A ragged blanket was draped over the back side, and I dragged it over the two of us.

I looked over at Mom and Grandma, who had both fallen asleep on the smaller of the couches, and were now knocked out, their bodies in contorted balls as they fought for room. I didn't want to wake them, though, so I enjoyed the extra space on my side, promising myself I'd let them have the better sleeping arrangements tomorrow. I clicked off the flashlight and stared up into the dark ceiling.

But sleep didn't come.

In the dark, all I could see was Brendan's face in my mind, staring up at me from the photographs in that album. He couldn't have known how things would all turn out. He had been cut off from the Fold, stuck here with no way to communicate, no way to ever ensure that his family would even know he had arrived safely. I wondered if he had ever sensed anything at all, any notion that things were getting worse back home. It hadn't seemed so. His efforts to return had waned over the years, and eventually he had completely abandoned even trying to get back to the Fold.

I tried to clear my own mind, tried to feel within me some sense of what was going on back on Aeso. Had there been any more battles? Was what remained of Stonemore's population able to remain hidden, as Kiron had hoped?

"Aster?" Cait's voice was small and lonely on the other side of the couch.

"Yeah?"

"How long until I can see Rhainn-y?"

I didn't answer, didn't know what to say. I might not be able to feel what was happening a universe away, but I could feel the pain and loneliness in the little girl on the other end of the sofa.

Finally, I made an attempt to answer.

"Soon, I think," I said. "We're going to find my dad. He has the gold we need. When we get it from him, we can all go back to Aeso together."

She laid quietly for a time, and I could tell she was turning over my words in her head. Finally, she responded.

"I don't want to go back to Aeso. Can you bring Rhainn-y back here? It's safer here."

Now it was my turn to be silent. The truth was, I didn't even know for sure if Rhainn was still alive. Though a part of me felt certain that he must be, that the Coyle and the Corentin must have realized that he was someone of importance to me. The good feelings that had made me feel so settled since coming into this falling down house suddenly evaporated as I imagined what uses they might put Rhainn to. To torment me. To hurt me. A prize I desperately wanted to their minds. An innocent kid I had promised to save to my mind.

"I think the best thing for now is that we all stick together," I said. Now that I was back with my family, I was starting to feel like I would never want to leave them again. I wondered what it would be like for them, landing on Aeso and facing the evil I knew awaited me. "But you're right, it is dangerous. I guess we'll have to wait and see." My eyes had slowly adjusted to the darkness, and the walls of the room, the trappings of a once safe life, started to come into view. "But listen. If it ends up that you have to come back with me, I'll hide you. Remember like how I hid you in that little cave? You were safe there, right?"

I could hear the smile in her voice as she said, "That was where I met Lissa and the cat."

I laughed. Pahana, the largest panther I'd ever seen, full of more magic than any other animal I had ever come into contact with, Cait simply referred to as a "cat."

"Yes," I said. "If you end up coming back with me, we'll hide you again."

"With Lissa?" she asked, and I was surprised by the hunger in her voice. I had always thought Larissa to be abrupt and terse.

"Sure, if that's what you want."

"Okay," she said. "I'll go."

We didn't talk again, and eventually I heard her breath become even and soft as she faded into sleep.

But I didn't.

The conversation had reminded me of my purpose here, to find the gold and then return as soon as possible. And I hadn't counted on having to face my father to do so.

Now it was his face that floated in the darkness above me, and hope combined with fear to swirl around in my stomach. It seemed like every step I took closer to him, I understood him less and less, and the desire I felt to see him again fought with the alarm bells going off in my head.

What would it be like, coming face to face? Would he be happy to see me? Or would he treat me like he had treated Grandma, brushing me aside as he went about his business?

I tried to imagine each scenario, prepare for how I might feel if any of those things happened, but then I realized that nothing would satisfy me. There was nothing he could do to make up for the rejection I had felt for so many years. But if he walked away from me again, proving me right wouldn't help me, either.

And then there was the other question, the newest one on the long list of things I wanted to learn the answers to.

Why had he hidden the map in the attic?

The sound of pattering rain started up again, and for a moment I looked around the room, half-expecting to see it pouring in. But as the deluge intensified, the structure stood strong, enough to protect us for the night, at least.

Suddenly, I felt like I understood a part of Jade I hadn't previously considered. She had wanted so desperately for Almara to comfort her, to take away all the misery in her heart that his own actions had created. But he hadn't been able to do that. At the very end, the way he looked at her before he leapt into the chasm, maybe he had understood. Maybe he had recognized both her and the mistakes he had made that had affected her so deeply.

Almara was gone now, and she would never know. She would never feel the closure of understanding his mind. She would never know if the man who leapt to his death did it to save his daughter, or if he had done it to stifle, once and for all, the dominating voices of his madness.

As I finally started to fall asleep, I wondered if I might get the chance that Jade had lost when Almara had leapt to his death. Maybe, when I finally found my father, I would know for certain whether he was truly insane. And if he would see me, as Almara had seemingly seen Jade in those last moments, as someone worth fighting for.

# CHAPTER EIGHT

"Noooo!"

I startled awake, staring around through a haze of sleep. The morning light came down through the opening in the staircase, a wide shaft shining into the dark basement.

Cait was breathing hard at the other end of the couch, gripped in what must have been a terrifying dream. Mom and Grandma were nowhere to be seen.

I sat up, grabbing one of her feet, trying to shake her awake, free her from her nightmare.

"No! Rhainn!" she yelled, her eyes squeezed shut.

She sat bolt upright, her fists clenching the rough blanket. She stared around in a panic, searching for her imaginary pursuer.

"It's okay," I said, patting her leg. "It was just a dream."

But my words weren't enough, and her eyes stared through me in a daze. She backed up against the armrest of the couch, clutching the blanket up to her chest as if I were about to attack.

"Cait, it's me. It's Aster."

A flicker of recognition flashed across her face, but the fear was too great, and it snuffed out the light. She opened her mouth and screamed.

"No!" I said, moving towards her. But my approach only made things worse. "Cait, it's just me!" Her screams were so loud I wasn't sure if she could hear me at all.

Mom thundered down the staircase. She stopped at the bottom, staring.

"What happened?" she asked.

I shrugged and started to answer, but she ignored me and raced over to Cait.

"Honey, honey," she cooed.

She moved around and sat on the couch facing her, her hands on her shoulders. Cait fought, tried to get away, her howls of fear only intensifying.

"Hey, now," Mom said. I was impressed she was able to stay so calm. My own heart was pounding about a thousand times a second. She wrapped her arms around Cait and pulled her close. "Everything's okay." Cait struggled against her grip, fighting for release. But Mom didn't falter. "You're safe here, honey," she went on. "Nothing bad is going to happen to you."

Slowly, Cait settled. I got up from the couch, still alarmed and wanting to help, but feeling useless. Mom gave me a look, not of rebuke, but of confusion.

"What happened?" she asked again.

"It was a nightmare, I think." My voice was winded, and I realized I was panting. I tried to slow my breath, to calm myself down. Cait had been looking at me as if I'd been the devil himself.

As her screaming ebbed and her breathing started to slow, the tears began. Soon she was sobbing like a baby in my mother's arms. Mom tucked her chin over Cait's head and slowly rocked her back and forth.

"It's okay now, baby," she said. "Everything's going to be okay."

I was amazed. How did Mom always know how to calm people down? I had tried to copy her, had traces of her within me as I had traveled with Jade and Rhainn and Cait. But just now, when I had been in a real panic, I had frozen up, unable to be of any help to anyone.

As my own breathing calmed, I knelt down beside them, putting one hand on Cait's back.

"Cait?"

Her sad blue eyes peeked out at me, but she immediately buried her face again.

"Cait, what happened?" I asked.

But whatever she had dreamed about had been too much for her. She melted into Mom, refusing to face me.

My heart clenched in my chest, hurt by her rejection.

What had she dreamt of?

Eventually, when it became clear that calming Cait was going to take a while, Mom looked up.

"Why don't you head upstairs with Grandma?" she said. "She's got some breakfast up there." She looked back down at the still trembling girl in her arms. "Don't worry," she said. "I'll take care of her."

I felt, oddly, that I had done something wrong. No, not just something wrong. Something terrible. Yet I had done nothing at all except fight back my own nightmares as the night had dragged on.

I turned, defeated, and headed towards the stairs.

Grandma was waiting at the top.

"What's going on down there?" she asked as I made my way up.

"Nightmare," I said, my eyes on my feet. I didn't want to talk about it, but not just because I hadn't been able to calm her myself.

It had been the way she had looked at me. With terror.

"Must have been some nightmare," she said as I brushed past her.

"Yeah," was all I said.

The kitchen, where yesterday it had been a disaster of corrosion and debris, was now unrecognizable. I stopped, staring.

"Your ma," Grandma said. "Chalk it up to nervous energy."

Mom had cleared off the debris from the kitchen counter and scrubbed it until it practically shone in the morning light. As I sat down on the single, half-broken stool, I could have been in any other suburban house. Except, of course, for the fact that the roof was missing over our heads. The sky above was clear and bright, and I breathed a sigh of relief at the knowledge that we would be traveling without the threat of rain, at least for a little while. That was one less thing Cait would have to worry about after the night she had had.

Laid out across the counter were a variety of breakfast options, all government issue. Grandma had survived so long out in the country mostly because she was able to grow much of her own food, and had developed a system for water purification that kept her independent. But she was still entitled to government rations just like every other citizen. Occasionally, the trucks would come through the countryside on their way between cities. As they made their way, the drivers all had a list of places to stop, smaller townships where there had been a few holdouts, people unwilling to give up everything in exchange from the protection the great buildings offered. My guess was that they had to make fewer and fewer stops as the years had gone by, but they were still willing to leave their boxes for Grandma at the end of the long gravel drive that led to the farm.

I had never eaten these with Grandma before; she had always cooked fresh food from scratch. She must have saved these rations up over the years, perfectly preserved in their foil-lined packaging. I sat down to a plate of sausage and eggs, with a side of freeze-dried berries for dessert. Meat was uncommon in the city, though not unheard of. Still, I was glad to have the sausage, and I vaguely wondered if it was actually a vegetable protein made to look and taste like meat.

In the city we ate a combination of foods like these, which were brought in from big factories that surrounded the most densely populated areas, and the fresh food produced by the growing towers that lined our streets. Every inch of the buildings that wasn't glass was covered with a solar film that took in the energy of the sun during the day and pumped it back through the interior systems at night, keeping the crops lit for twenty four hours straight. I had once taken a school field trip inside one of the massive buildings to learn about how our food was grown, and I had been astounded by the labyrinth of hydroponic tubes that seemed to stretch for miles in a twisted mass. Tomatoes. Strawberries. Floor after floor of salad greens and soybeans. And all of it protected from the rain and the pollution of the outside world.

The towers were our lives. Without them, the entire population would starve. It used to be that the higher up you lived in a building, the wealthier you had to be. But no longer. Now, the tall buildings that had once housed banks and businesses and penthouses were all designated for growing food, and the people lived in the shade down below.

Grandma finished up her own breakfast as I was starting mine, and I watched her draw out a towel from the back of a drawer and start cleaning her plate with it. Then, as if she were tidying up back home, she opened one of the few standing cabinets and stacked it neatly where she had found it. She turned back with the towel and began wiping the crumbs she had created off the counter. When she glanced up to check that I was eating, she caught my eye, realizing I had been watching her.

"You never know," she said, shrugging. "May as well not trash the place just because we stayed here a night. Could be some other traveler needs these things again someday."

She had a point, and yet the chances of such a situation ever occurring again in the future were so slim I still wondered what compelled her to do it. I guess it was just her habits, ingrained within her after so many decades of performing the same actions again and again, no matter the circumstances.

The stairs creaked and I whipped around in my seat. Mom had Cait's hand in hers, and Cait's eyes darted around the room as her head cleared the banister. When she saw me, she froze. Mom leaned down, whispering to her, and whatever she said must have convinced her, because she started climbing again.

I slid out of my seat, taking my plate to the other end of the counter and leaving the space open for Cait to sit down. She climbed up on the rungs of the chair and sat, refusing to look me in the eye.

Grandma looked back and forth between the two of us, her confusion returning.

"There," Mom said, breathing an audible sigh of relief. I got the impression it had been no easy feat to convince Cait to accompany her back into my presence. "Cathy, can you get Cait a plate of food?"

Grandma seemed to shake herself out of her thoughts, and a moment later Cait was presented with the same breakfast I had been. Grandma didn't ask further questions, which I was grateful for. Instead, she directed the conversation elsewhere, leaning back against the far counter and sipping from a mug of what had to be government issue coffee.

"We're about four hours out, I'd say," she said.

Mom nodded, taking the last little bit of sausage from the serving plate and popping it into her mouth. She eyeballed Cait.

"Do you want the first shift or shall I take it?" Grandma asked, trying again.

"I'll drive," Mom said, chewing thoughtfully. "I remember the way. It wasn't that long ago that I came through here."

That's right. Mom had been through Denver just a few months back, searching for Dad

"How did you find him anyways?" I asked. "The first time."

Her gaze shifted from Cait's face to mine.

"It was his old friend from college, Duncan," she said. "You never knew him, but he worked for many years with your father. Occasionally, he and I would touch base, trade information about Jack and you. Jack would sometimes turn up to see Duncan, always without warning, so we tried to stay in touch in case he came through. Always wanted to keep him updated."

I knew Mom must have always hoped that, if she were able to get information to Dad about my condition, that he might return. That the idea of his sick son, battling against disease without him by his side, would be enough to put him back on track. Back on his meds. Back to reality.

But, of course, he never had shown up. Not to check on me. Not to inquire. I guessed that whatever information this Duncan had been passing along to Dad through the years hadn't made a dent in his resolve to stay away.

"Duncan always knew where to find your father, better than anyone else at least," she continued. "He told me that Jack had settled above Denver in an abandoned house. Though why anyone would ever *choose* to live at that elevation is beyond me. He would only return on occasion to take his collected rations."

I thought about this as I picked at my eggs. I had never known where Dad had gone, only that he wasn't with us anymore. Now that I found out he had been living in Denver all this time, his behavior made even less sense. It was crazy of him to stay in Denver. It was right at the altitude where the majority of the poisoned atmosphere had settled, like a fog of smog that had hung right around five thousand feet for the past thirty years. The city itself had been abandoned long ago.

So why would he stay? Why choose a ghost town to make your home in? And it wasn't only a ghost town. It was a place that would eventually kill him as the toxins in the air slowly built up in his system.

It didn't make any sense.

After it became clear that Cait had little intention of eating, Mom cleared away the food and finished the tidying Grandma had begun, so that when we were ready to leave the place fifteen minutes later, it was as clean as it had been in probably thirty years. Grandma led the way as we stepped out into the morning, ready to move on.

The neighborhood was even spookier during the day than it had been at night, and immediately my skin began tingling with nerves. The crumbling houses, once the homes of countless citizens, now looked as though a bomb had gone off nearby. Walls were eroded after years of rain exposure. Roofs were collapsed in almost every case. The street was cracked and littered with potholes, and not a single blade of vegetation remained among the once-tended garden beds.

The winter breeze ruffled my hair and sent chills running down my back. I headed straight for the car door, the temporary comfort of staying in the basement room forgotten. I was ready to leave.

Mom brought Cait around to her side of the car. Cait whined, clearly still afraid of me. She shot me nervous looks through the window glass in between her protests. For a moment I kept my door cracked open, listening. But I quickly decided I didn't want to hear any more, and I snapped it shut, muffling the sound of their argument.

Finally, with the authority I knew only too well, Mom had had enough. She opened the side door and pointed an impatient finger at the seat beside me. Cait must have understood that she was out of options, because she went silent as soon as she realized I could hear her again, and obediently climbed in. She sat as far away from me as possible, staring out the window like a dog in a cage, desperate to be free.

Mom and Grandma opened their doors and got in, and a minute later we were bumping along down the road on our way out of the destroyed neighborhood.

I stared out the window, just like Cait did, at once trying to take in the devastation around me and trying to figure out how to reach her again. I had had my own fair share of horrifying dreams, most of which had come to me since I had first been pulled into the Fold. But I had never had a dream that frightened me of the people I surrounded myself with whom I *knew* to be good. Cait didn't seem able to recognize, or even remember, that we had been buddies just hours ago. An unpleasant feeling of shame, undeserved and confusing, washed through me. And it was joined by anger at being so quickly tossed aside, labeled by this little kid as something evil, based on nothing more than a bad dream.

I looked over to her. She had cracked her window a few inches, and stared out of the moving car with a determination I hadn't seen in her face before. Had she decided, then? I was now someone she could never trust again? She glanced over at me, fear immediately returning to her face, and my anger faltered. She was still just a kid. I tried to smile.

"Hey," I said, trying to catch her eye. "What has your favorite food been since you got here?"

She didn't answer at first, but when she looked up at my question, her eyes stayed with mine this time.

"My favorite so far has been the spaghetti," I said. I puckered my lips, pretending to slurp up a long, saucy strand of the stuff.

Her eyes flickered, and a hint of a smile flashed across her face.

"Was your favorite the spaghetti, too?" I asked.

The fear on her face seemed to retreat a notch, and she nodded.

"Yeah, I thought so," I said, looking up towards the front of the car. "Grandma makes a mean plate of spaghetti."

Mom and Grandma chuckled from the front seat.

"How can spaghetti be mean?" Cait asked, her voice tiny. It was the first time she had spoken to me since the dream.

Relief flooded through me. I smiled, glad that I hadn't let my anger outweigh the obligation I had to her, to keep her safe. My own feelings could wait. As I well knew, sometimes the worst nightmares seemed an awful lot like reality.

I turned back to her to explain as Mom turned the car back onto the highway, thundering down the road towards the place and man we hoped held our answers.

# CHAPTER NINE

Mom stopped the car before we made the final ascent to Denver. We all got out and stretched. Grandma fetched us each a drink from the water barrels, and Mom filled the tank with gasoline from the handheld cans. The wind was greater here, and not far above our heads the thick, brown smog that blanketed the plains of Colorado stretched out, all but blocking the mountain vistas in the distance. This would be our last fresh air until we got Dad and got out of here.

My stomach dropped for what felt like the hundredth time today. This could be it, the day I saw him again. The day I might find out some answers to the growing list of questions I had. The day I looked, not for the first time, into Corentin eyes.

Cait had calmed down considerably, though every once in a while I would still catch her looking at me out of the corner of her eye. It was almost as if she expected me to morph into a demon at any second, and now she was just keeping watch, ready to flee when the inevitable happened.

I walked away down the road a little bit, kicking rocks that lined the pavement as I went. Another time, during what felt like another life, I would have been thrilled to be headed towards Denver. Not because of Denver, itself, but because it would mean I'd be so near to the mountains. Up there above the acid haze I had always felt certain I would be allowed to be a kid. A normal kid in a normal place, where the air was clean and the rain didn't sear your skin. Instead of a sick kid in a polluted world, where everyone was focused on basic survival, not play.

But now the time for play was over. Those dreams I had had of romping through the wilderness, playing games with sticks and rocks, pretending to have magic, had been replaced by the real thing. I wasn't sure I would ever be able to play again.

I was starting to feel like this whole plan was unraveling, even though the journey had just begun. Cait's behavior had unnerved me, and seeing the destruction of the towns we passed by made me squirm with unease. So much had happened here, so much had changed for the humans of Earth in so little a time. I wondered why the Corentin hadn't wrecked the planets in the Triaden like he had done to Earth. But then, maybe he didn't have such fine control over everything that happened. Maybe his intentions were all that mattered, bringing out the different evils that each place had within them already.

Mom called from down the road, and I turned to rejoin them. The three of them sat ready in the car, the motor running. Someone had produced strips of cloth, like bandanas but made from whatever Grandma had lying around. Mom and Grandma had theirs tied around their mouths and noses, staring determinedly at the road ahead. In the backseat, Cait was already trying to remove hers, pulling it down disobediently so that her nose was free.

I slid into my seat and took the cloth from Mom's hand dangling over the backseat.

"Will this really help?" I asked. I stared at it, and then at Cait. Like her, I didn't want to put this old stinky rag over my face, and when I did, it reminded me of the claustrophobic feeling of having an oxygen mask strapped to my head in the hospital.

"The less of this crud you get in your lungs, the better," Grandma said. It was her turn in the driver's seat, and as soon as she was satisfied that the cloth was secured around my face, she hit the gas and the car sped forward with a lurch. My stomach lurched along with it as we sped towards my father.

I looked over at Cait, but her eyes were back on the road again. As the car bumped along the road, she quietly sang a tune I hadn't heard before.

*"The child of Elyso looks at me*
*The child of Elyso sees my dreams*
*Through wind and rain and swirling hail*
*The child of Elyso finds the trail*

*The child of Elyso knows the dark*
*She maps the night and follows spark*
*Her eyes see past the cloud of day*
*The child of Elyso knows the way"*

"What is that song?" I asked, intrigued. I had long found the songs and stories of the Triaden both fascinating and useful. They were usually filled with small details about the past that were often left out of normal speech.

"Just a song my Ma used to sing to me," she said, her gaze still fixed on the horizon. "It's about me."

I smiled.

"A song about a magical child was written just for you, eh?" I asked.

She glanced at me, noting the smirk on my face as I teased her. She did not return the smile.

"You'll see," she said, turning back to the window view again.

It seemed our moment of connection was over. I looked out my window, too. As the car slowly ascended, the mountains became clearer, a range of vibrant green peaks muddied by the acid veil, but still spectacular. Even through the haze, they were beautiful, the green of the trees cutting off in an abrupt line at the spot where the rains became polluted. No clouds threatened the sky today, though. Any baby greens trying to push their way up from the earth would be spared for at least another day until more rain collected far above.

We were all silent for nearly the whole ride, Cait eventually falling asleep with her forehead resting on the window. Her cloth had slid down, exposing her upper lip. I thought about straightening it for her, but after the last time she had woken up, I didn't want to risk it.

I leaned my own head against the glass, watched the landscape slip away as the car sped up the incline.

A couple hours. That was all it took. The giant buildings of Denver loomed on the horizon, rising up like the mountains behind them. Only the mountains weren't crumbling. The road widened until it was five lanes in either direction, an unusual sight without a single other vehicle to share it with. We didn't stop, didn't dare take any extra time at this elevation to see what remained of the once thriving place.

The city was like no place I had ever seen. Everywhere, the signs of technology were present. In the buildings. In the streets. In the vestiges of billboards the peeked out at us from nearly every corner.

But it was just as dead as the other places we had been. Huge swaths of graffiti were painted on walls and pillars. Some warned people to get out of town while they still had a chance. Others, once vibrant with the colors in the artists' visions, were like one last cry, documenting history onto the tall structures to remain for all time. Glass littered the streets, blown out by the weather or movements of the Earth, or maybe by the frustrated citizens as they left their homes for safer elevations.

I rolled down the window and stuck my head partway out, gazing at the buildings as we passed them by one by one, like giant trees stretching towards the sky above. The pollution was visible in the air five feet in front of our faces, tiny particles of floating exhaust, collected over centuries, now come to rest in this sick, brown layer that killed everything in its path. And it seemed endless. No matter how much the rain came, it was never enough to bring the layer down. I tightened the cloth over my face and turned to find Cait, now wide awake, doing the same.

"What are they?" she called as we passed by the towers, once so grand and magnificent.

"They're like really big houses," Grandma answered from the front. I was impressed. She seemed to be catching onto the fact that certain things, so familiar to the rest of us, were unusual, and even frightening, for Cait.

"Where are the people?" she asked.

"They left a long time ago," Grandma said. "Close up your windows, kids. It can't be good for you."

We did as we were told, bringing our heads back inside the car and watching the rest of the city from within the frames of our window panes.

But Denver was gone in a flash as we sped by, and soon we were rocketing through the suburbs on the other side, mountainbound.

After a while, I found I didn't want to look out the window any longer. Cait must have felt the same, because I found her slumped in her seat, staring blankly towards the interior of the car. I felt like I understood her, even though we didn't speak. I didn't want to see any more rows of homes decimated by decades of rain and decay any more than she did.

I must have fallen asleep, because the next thing I knew, we were slowing down. My head felt light and dizzy as I stared around, trying to get my bearings.

"I don't feel…right," I said to no one in particular.

"It's the haze," Mom said, her voice sort of croaky. She and Grandma had switched while I slept, and now she sat hunched over the steering wheel, rubbing her eyes every few seconds. "There's a reason people left this place."

I stared out the window and found that we were now on the doorstep of the mountains. What had looked majestic and grand from afar was now enormous and oppressive as I stared up at the peaks above, now clearly visible despite the fog.

It didn't take Mom long to find the turn; she had been here not long ago, and I guess she remembered the way. She pulled the car off the road onto a gravel drive, the tires crunching and bumping as we made our way down it towards the base of the mountain. Finally, she stopped, and for a moment I was confused as to why.

But then I saw it. Hidden between a swath of dead timber, a small hunter's cabin stood stubbornly erect. The metal roof nailed to the top was what had saved it all these years, I guessed, though the rest of the place was a wreck.

She turned to Grandma.

"You ready?" she asked.

*Grandma?* What about me?

My stomach was doing flips as I crawled out onto the rocky ground. Apparently, I wasn't the only one affected by the haze. Every one of us had to lean against the side of the car as our swimming brains got used to standing again. Mom was the first to get her balance back, and she stumbled towards the house. Part of me wanted to call to her, to demand that she stop and let me go first, somehow thinking that my experience with Jade while she was possessed somehow qualified me above the others to deal with whatever waited on the other side of that door.

But the truth was, I had never been so terrified in my life. Not when facing Jade. Not when facing the Coyle. Inside that tiny house could be my worst nightmare. Or even more frightening, what if he was waiting for me, sane after all this time?

Mom staggered up to the door and rapped on the wood.

"Jack!" she called. "Jack, open the door!"

I looked around, wondering how he could survive in a place like this. Why he would want to.

Finally, when it became clear nobody was going to answer, Mom pushed open the door.

"Jack we're coming in," she called.

But she may as well have been talking to herself. As we all took the first steps into the tiny space, the truth became apparent.

He wasn't there waiting to kill me. Or waiting to guard his gold against me. Or even talk to me.

He wasn't there at all.

The cabin was empty.

# CHAPTER TEN

"What do we do now?" I asked, hoping that someone other than me had some sort of idea.

Mom leaned against the small table, clearly exhausted. All of us were having trouble breathing.

"Ha!" Grandma said. "Look at this!"

She walked over to the kitchen sink and flicked a switch on the wall. A whirring sound came out of a machine that was mounted into the one small window the tiny cabin had. Grandma shuffled Cait inside and shut the door behind her. Then she removed her bandana and stood in front of the machine, breathing deeply.

"What is it?" I asked.

"An air purifier," she said. "I remember when these things first came out, back when people were hoping the haze would eventually come down. Here, come over." She gestured at us to join her, and soon all four of us stood with our faces pressed up against it like little kids in front of an air conditioner on a hot summer day. Immediately, my swimming brain started to settle as I breathed in the untainted oxygen.

Eventually, we all settled back into the room. A single chair sat before the tiny dining table, and a loveseat provided seating for the rest of us. None of us seemed eager to get moving again, back outside where just breathing was painful. Finally, it was Mom who broke the silence.

"There's a village up the road," she said. "I think we should go there next, see if they know anything. I don't think it's too far. Jack mentioned buying supplies up there once. Maybe they know where he is."

"You mean, people really do still live in this?" I gestured out the window to the haze beyond.

"I think it's above it," she said. "It's a steep incline from here."

She began fumbling with her bandana again and tied it back over her face.

"You ready?" she asked. "I'd just as soon get out of this."

As much as I dreaded walking back out into the haze, the wonderful feeling of having pure oxygen coursing through my lungs again had invigorated me. I looked down at Cait as I tied my own bandana back on.

"You ready to go?" I asked. "It won't be long."

Cait looked miserable. It seemed every moment she spent in this strange world, her situation became more difficult. I saw her lower lip begin to stick out, and before it could start to tremble I knelt down before her.

"Soon, real soon, we'll be above the haze. Everything will be clean up there. The air. The rain. We'll get to take a nice break, okay?"

For the first time since her nightmare, her eyes locked onto mine. She tucked her lip back under again and nodded.

We made it back to the car, this time staying fully upright. I had to fight the impulse to hold my breath for the next half hour as the car wound its way up through the mountains.

As I stared out across the beginning of the mountain range, the scenery changed dramatically. First, the haze became thicker, and I clapped my hands to my face, fearful that the poisoning my body was already fighting was about to increase. Then, something caught my eye, and I gasped.

Snow.

Up front, both Mom and Grandma sucked in their breath, clearly surprised. From down in the valley below we could barely see the tops of the mountains, and what we could see was stained brown by the haze. We hadn't expected snow.

As we ascended, more and more could be seen scattered across the dead earth. Something loomed in the distance a little farther up, but I couldn't make out what it was through the thick, gaseous layer.

And then, all at once, the haze disappeared. And I saw it.

Trees.

I had never seen trees before. Not like this. Not on Earth. The thin patch of grass that was carefully kept alive by those who ran the city was the extent of my experience with things that grew in the natural world.

But here, everywhere, the forest rested atop the mountains like a thick, protective blanket.

We had burst through the topmost layer of poison that lay across our world, and the sun shone brightly against the stark white snowdrifts lining the road. A thin dusting of snow rested atop the pine boughs, and the sharp smell of the trees immediately perfumed the interior of the car.

Mom slowed, and her eyes widened with something like wonder.

"Whoa," she said under her breath.

In the front seat, I heard a sniffling sound, and I realized Grandma was crying, faced with a memory of what her life had once been like. Her life and that of so many others.

"Never thought I'd see snow again," she said, yanking off her bandana and pulling a handkerchief from her purse, blowing her nose.

"Never thought I'd see snow at all," Mom said, staring awestruck at the peaks above.

They looked at each other and laughed, a kind of choking sound as it came through their tears.

"You've never seen snow?" I asked.

"You *have?*" she said.

I laughed, too.

"Not here," I said, remembering the snow planet I had found myself on so long ago. That was the first time I had ever come into contact with the animals of the White Guard. At the memory of the giant wolf who had saved me from the predators of that place, I searched the treeline, hoping childishly to see some hint that their protection had somehow followed me back to Earth.

"Well, I haven't," she said, leaning forward against the steering wheel so she could look up at the looming mountains.

I pulled my face cloth down and reached over to help Cait with hers, but it was already off. She sat with her back fully to me, her face glued to the window as the trees passed by.

Finally, when Mom started moving the car up the mountain again, we each rolled down our windows, all of us but mom sticking our heads out like dogs, sucking in the cold, clean mountain air.

The light that came down from above was sharper, crisper, than what hit below the pollution. I turned as we continued upwards past it and saw the haze lying there like a sticky film over the Earth.

Within five minutes of coming through the haze, the road gave a sharp turn to the left, and we saw a smattering of buildings dotted along the hillsides. This was the village Mom had been talking about. From inside the little dwellings, curtains shifted and curious eyes peeked through the windows. She pulled over when she reached a little store. No signs hung in front, but there was something more lively about the place than the other buildings, and several people could be seen staring curiously out through the thick glass windows.

Together, we all exited the car. Immediately we were struck by the frigid air, and looking over I found Cait already shivering. We quickly made our way inside, a tiny bell tinkling at the opening of the door. The place was cramped, but warm, and I was grateful for the heat when the door shut behind us with a thunk.

"Hello, there, stranger," a man said. He stood behind a small counter, clearly indicating this was his place. Three others sat on barstools facing him, two with bowls of steaming soup set before them. They watched their friend carefully as he came out from behind and outstretched a hand. "Don't usually see new folks come through these parts. I'm Amos."

Mom took his hand and smiled, her face genuinely pleased. There was something about this man that was comforting, and not just to her. He was older, with white speckled hair and a scruffy beard, but nowhere near Grandma's age. And he was unmistakably in control around here. Yet his eyes were soft and kind, and I felt relief wash through me at having come upon such friendly folk.

"I'm Dana," Mom said, shaking his hand. "This is Cathy, my son Aster, and our friend Cait." She gestured to each of us in turn.

"Nice to meet you, Dana," he said. "What brings you all the way up here?"

Mom's face darkened just a bit.

"We're looking for someone. His name is Jack Wood. I'm hoping you've seen him around here before. He's a little...odd."

"Well, like I said, not too many folks come through these parts," Amos said. "He's odd, how?"

"He's ill," Mom said, her eyes never wavering from the man's face. "He sees things that aren't there. Talks to himself a lot."

*Just say he's crazy,* I thought.

But she stayed diplomatic in her description of my father.

"He usually lives down below in a little cabin, inside the haze layer," she continued. "But when we went there looking for him, he was gone."

"Ah, you're talking about the hermit," Amos said. "Didn't know his name was Jack. Yeah, we don't see much of him around here. He sticks to down below, usually. The one to help you there is Sean." He stepped back and gestured to an older boy sitting at the counter, the one without the soup. "Sean's pa works the mines down below, and I know he's seen the hermit, or I should say Jack, before."

Sean stood up from the table and walked over to Mom.

"Hello," he said. He outstretched his hand with a confidence that was both forced and impressive. He couldn't be older than sixteen, and yet he was obviously used to operating in the adult world at this stage of his life. Or he was trying to, at least.

"Nice to meet you, Sean," Mom said, shaking his hand in turn. "Do you know where we can find him?"

"He's probably down in the mine with Dad," he said. "I've heard about him plenty of times. But we don't have any way to get down there." He peered out the window at the sedan. "That car reliable?"

Mom looked over her shoulder, shrugging.

"Well, it got us this far up the mountain," she said.

"Haven't seen Dad in a few weeks," he said. "Usually he gets a ride up the hill with the food transport, but he wasn't on the last truck. I'd sure appreciate a ride down and back. We were just talking about a plan to go down and find out if everything's okay."

"Of course," Mom said. "There's plenty of room for all of us."

Sean turned back to Amos.

"You'll tell Caleb and Lily where I've gone?" he asked. Amos nodded. "Make sure to tell him to keep up on his chores, too."

Amos laughed.

"You got that boy working too hard, Sean," he said. "He's just a kid."

Sean shrugged.

"Doesn't matter if he's a kid," he said. "He's still gotta work just like the rest of us."

Amos shook his head, a flash of sadness steeling across his face.

"It's a different world now," Grandma said to him, smiling gently.

"That it is, ma'am," Amos said.

Cait tugged at my pant leg, and I knelt down, meeting her gaze.

"You said it would be over by now," she said, her voice betraying just a hint of a whine. "I don't want to go back down."

"The lass can stay up here with us, if you like," Amos said, smiling down at Cait. "Up at Sean's place there's even a playmate for her."

I didn't like that idea, of leaving Cait so quickly with unknown people we had only met five minutes ago. Clearly, Cait didn't think much of this idea, either. She moved around and hid behind me, as if worried that Amos would force her to stay.

"No," she whispered. "Don't leave me here."

I sensed no ill will on the part of Amos and the other men in the place, but I couldn't blame Cait for her nervousness. Even I, much older than she was, would have been on edge being abandoned for what could be days with a group of strangers. I turned to face her again.

"I know I said we'd be out of the haze," I said. "I didn't realize we'd have to go back down so quickly. We won't be long down below. But I think you're right. We should stick together. That's what I promised, right?"

She nodded, taking a deep breath and blowing it out, steeling herself for what was to come.

Sean moved over to the door and took down a big, puffy jacket. He wrapped himself in it and flipped up the fur-lined hood over his short-cropped, black hair.

"Back in a few days, I expect," he said.

Cait gave a small huff at this. I wasn't thrilled either, but I kept my silence.

"Don't worry," Sean said, more to Mom and Grandma than to the rest of us. "The mine has pretty clean air. It's just getting back down the mountain that's difficult."

He opened the door and led the way back out to the car. Mom opened the driver's side and Grandma moved to sit in the back with us.

"That's alright, ma'am," Sean said. "Anyone who's survived as long as you has earned a front seat ride down into the haze." He gave a flicker of a smile, but it was gone from his face nearly as quickly as it had arrived. Grandma exchanged looks with Mom.

"Well, that'll be fine with me, son," she said, opening her car door.

The three of us squeezed into the back, Sean in a window seat and Cait between us. Mom turned on the car and flicked on the heat, and soon we could no longer see our breath from within the tiny space. She turned the wheel, and together we headed back down the mountain, into the haze and the unknown meeting below.

# CHAPTER ELEVEN

As we pierced back through the haze, none of us needed reminding; we all reached for our bandanas, wrapping them tightly around our faces. Sean, who was used to living so close to the chemicals, produced his own face wrap from the inside pocket of his coat. He looked out the window as we descended, and soon we passed by the little cabin where our search had begun.

"It's not far from here," Sean said. "Keep an eye out for a little road off to the left. It's pretty hidden."

Within a minute, his eyes fell onto a patch of earth that was more packed down than the rest.

"There," he said, pointing.

Mom turned the car down the old, forgotten road. Twigs scratched against the windows where the trees had grown over into the path, what was left of the branches still sticking out in the spots more protected from the rain. The road wasn't long, and soon we pulled up before what looked like an old, abandoned mine.

A tunnel was carved into the face of the rock, braced on all sides by beams of wood as thick as tree trunks. Mom killed the engine.

"Okay," she said. "You say the air is clean below?"

"Yes, ma'am," he said. "Not so clean as in the village above, but clean enough to breathe." He adjusted his face mask over his nose.

Together, we all got out of the car. Mom made a beeline for the cave entrance, but I was relieved to find that we hadn't been in the haze long enough to have too bad an effect on our lungs. I wasn't dizzy like I had been before, though I instinctively longed for the clean air below.

Grandma and Cait walked up beside us, Cait hid behind Grandma's legs, peering out nervously. Mom held out the one flashlight she had dug out of the car to Sean, and he took the first steps into the cave. We all followed.

I felt Cait's little hand slip into mine. I took a deep breath.

I was here for my gold, nothing more. He had stolen it from the family home, Brendan's home, and now I was about to take it back and use it how Brendan had always intended.

My feet wanted to walk on ahead, move faster, get this all over with so I could be on my way. But we only had the one flashlight, and I was forced by the rest of the group to move slowly. It was agony as they took careful step after careful step, while I wanted nothing more than to run. It wasn't until Grandma stopped walking and yelped with pain that I snapped out of my focused pursuit of my father.

"Ouch!" she said, her voice echoing off the slick rock walls. She had knocked her forehead against a low hanging chunk of rock, and when Mom carefully removed her hand from covering it, I saw a small cut an inch long just above her eyebrow.

Mom untied the face cloth from behind her neck, then walked around behind Grandma and fiddled with the knot on her cloth. I stopped and spun Cait around and started to work on hers. But I shouldn't have bothered. Before I had even begun to undo the knot, she had yanked the thing down below her chin, exposing her face. I followed her example, finding immediate, unexpected relief in the clean air of the mountain cavern as it cooled my face, which had grown sweaty beneath the fabric.

Mom dabbed at the cut, but then Grandma shooed her away, taking the cloth from her.

"I'm not a child, Dana," she said, brushing past her and farther into the cave. When Mom stared after her, surprised, she turned back. "You coming?"

I smiled despite the momentary tension and exchanged a look with Mom. She sure was a tough old lady. Sean had continued on without us, and we shuffled along to catch up.

We all moved down into the mine, and the farther down we went, the warmer the air became. I didn't mind, though. As long as I could breathe, any air temperature was fine by me.

"How far is it?" I asked.

"Not far," Sean said.

Ahead, an old mine cart stood in our way, long abandoned along the tracks we were following. I touched its edges as I passed, squeezing between it and the wall of the shaft. The wood was still in good shape after what must have been decades, maybe centuries. My confidence in Mom's judgement about the air increased tenfold upon seeing the good repair the cart was in, and I breathed deeply, trying to fill myself up with it before we had to go back out into the haze.

My confidence in Sean, though, was not so high.

I had spent more than my fair share of time inside caves and caverns in the Triaden, but something about this one felt different. Not necessarily menacing. But dead. I might have expected to see streaks of gold along the walls and ceiling of the place, hints about the treasure hidden within the mountain. But all that greeted my eyes was dry, brown stone, not a hint of shimmer anywhere.

I nudged Grandma in the darkness.

"How do we know we can trust him?" I asked. Something about being led into a dark mountain by a total stranger wasn't sitting right with me. I had seen too many dark mountains.

She shrugged.

"We don't," she whispered. "But what choice do we have? We just have to hope that the goodness in people is still alive in this part of the world."

Hope.

It was not an unfamiliar concept to me.

My worry over Sean faded away as we continued deeper and deeper, replaced with a nervousness so encompassing, my hands were starting to shake with it. It wouldn't be long now. Any minute I would be standing face to face with my father.

*Boom. Boom. Boom.*

It was the sound I imagined my heart making in my chest. The sound of years of rejection. Of loneliness. Of apprehension.

*Boom. Boom. Boom.*

I shook myself out of my stupor and realized the sound wasn't just coming from inside my head. There was actually an echo drifting up through the cave. Mom sped up, her jaw locked tight, her face determined and as harsh as I had ever seen it.

This was it.

I was barely breathing, yet my body did as I instructed. My legs moved, my feet found purchase on the slick floor.

And then we turned, and what I saw took what remained of my breath away.

The tunnel opened up into a cavern that loomed far above our heads. Sean shined the flashlight across the space, revealing a gigantic underground lake, as still as a sheet of glass, within the mountain.

"Whoa," I breathed.

But he didn't stop. On the far side of the cavern, a light shone against one wall, and the figure of a man stood before it, pounding what looked like a sledgehammer into a hole in the ground.

*Boom. Boom. Boom.*

The world around me seemed to blur with every step I took towards him, and part of me felt sure that I wouldn't remember whatever it was I was preparing to say. Up until this moment, I hadn't really thought about just how I was going to convince him to hand over the gold. I had thought, childishly, that he would just give it to me. That, upon seeing the son he had been without for so long, he would be inspired to help my cause.

It was too late now. Each step I took brought me closer and closer to him. Mom paused, waiting for me, and wrapped her arm around my shoulder, pushing me slightly ahead of her.

"Jack," she called ahead.

I froze, but she pushed me onward. Terror suddenly gripped me, and I felt like a five-year-old kid again, watching my father as he put his madness through its paces. Watching him as he shouted at demons only he could see. Watching him as he fled our apartment, our lives, without so much as a suitcase or even a backward glance.

She must have felt my hesitation, but she didn't let me falter.

"It'll be okay," she whispered.

*Boom. Boom. Boom.*

*Stop it! Stop it!*

We were fifteen feet away now. Then ten. Then five.

"Jack!" she yelled, cutting through the noise of the hammer.

He stopped his pounding and turned. The headlamp he wore over his face temporarily blinded us, and for a moment all I could see was the round, white light as it bobbed in front of my vision. Then, seemingly understanding, he removed it, shining it towards the ground, instead.

Mom pushed me a little, and I took a few tentative steps forward. Red shadows from the white light remained over my sight, and I blinked, trying to readjust to the faint light in the cave.

"Dad?" I asked. My voice had gone unusually quiet, and I cleared my throat, getting ready for the conversation that must come next.

He stepped closer, and suddenly we were face to face, just a few feet away from each other. He raised up his arm, and I thought he was going to hit me. But it was the hand with the light in it, and he shined now on the wall, bouncing it, casting his face in a soft, dim glow.

And all the air I had been holding in came pouring out of my lungs like a deflating balloon.

We had been right. There *was* a man in this cave.

But he was not my father.

# CHAPTER TWELVE

"Dad!" Sean said, launching towards his father, his adult pretense temporarily forgotten.

The man staggered backwards, surprised by the sudden appearance of his son amidst a group of strangers.

"Sean?" he asked. "What are you doing here?"

Sean broke apart from his father and looked up into his dirty face.

"These folks came through town looking for the hermit," he said. "I brought them down here to try to help out." He paused, standing tall again, his maturity, still clearly new to him, returning. "We've been worried about you."

"Worried about me?" the man said. "Naw."

I stared around the cavern, searching for "the hermit."

"Is Jack here?" Mom asked, interrupting the reunion. "We went to the cabin, and no one has seen him in your village."

"Jack?" he asked. "Who, the crazy guy? No. He left a few weeks back."

I looked back at him, unbelieving.

He had slipped through our fingers again.

I took a couple steps to one side and leaned against the wall, defeated.

My father wasn't here.

The man looked around at the group of us, taking time to inspect one face after another, his own looking perplexed.

"What are you all doing this far out?" he asked. "It ain't safe at this elevation, you know."

He was tall, much taller than he had appeared from afar. And big. Not fat, but wide and muscular, as though he had spent every day of his life working the earth. His skin was a deep brown, and his black hair hung down his back in a fat braid.

I opened my mouth to speak, but nothing came out.

"We're looking for Jack Wood," Mom said, taking over. "He used to…live here." She cast a nervous glance around the cavern, as if expecting him to jump out and frighten her at any moment.

"He don't no more," he said. He had a short piece of wood in his mouth, and he chewed the tip of it as he talked, moving it back and forth from one corner of his mouth to the other. "Flipped out when I got here a few weeks back. Said I was a demon or somethin'. Then took off. You friends of his?"

"Family," Mom said.

The man nodded, as if no further explanation was needed. We were the family of the crazy man, come to fetch him from his mountain asylum.

"Do you know where we can find him?" she asked, her face visibly disappointed. No, irritated. It was just one more time she had to follow him along insanity's trail.

The man shrugged.

"He was yabberin' on about California before he left. Tried to taunt me, tellin' me I'd never have the strength to make it that far. Threatened me, even, before he finally packed up his gear. I won't lie. I'd been hoping to find company in these old mines, but I didn't shed a tear when he moved along."

"How would he get to California?" I was surprised to hear my own voice asking this question. I had seen the prominent gold band encircling the spot in California. He must have seen it, too.

"He told me he was going hunting in the mountains," he said. "As to how he planned to make it there, you got me."

"Hunting?" I asked.

"Hunting for gold, I expect," he said. "Though there ain't no one to sell to in California. The Rockies are the edge of civilization now. Nothin' left out west. Still, I suppose, if you knew where to look, and you had a way to travel, a fella could make a living. Maybe better." His eyes got a faraway look for a moment, as if he were considering the prospect of further riches if he were to do his hunting out west.

"Make a living?" I asked. Who on Earth would care about gold anymore?

"Sure," he said, hoisting the sledgehammer over his shoulder. "There ain't much left in this mountain, but if you work at it you can find enough to feed a family." He smiled down at Sean and ruffled his short hair with one of his brawny hands. Then, turning back to me, he must have seen the surprised look on my face, because he continued. "What, you think cause the world's gone to hell that there ain't no market left for gold? Sure there is, especially seeing as most folks only care about city life nowadays. Ain't nobody left who wants to get out here and really get their hands dirty. But there'll always be a need for gold. Energy.

Antibiotics. For some who can still afford it, jewelry. You find enough of it and you can make a nice little life for yourself."

"But who do you sell it to?" I asked. I tried to imagine finding other people way out here, where the Earth was so scorched it couldn't have supported a population even if the rain *wasn't* poisoned. A rock of gold would be as useless as any other at helping people to survive in a situation like this.

"They come through every once in a while, the government vans. They trade us clothing and sugar, other supplies we can't get on our own, for the gold we find. Of course, we get our rations just like everyone else, too. Though I think not for much longer. I think Uncle Sam might be getting tired of trekkin' all the way out here to give us our mylar bags of stew."

I turned to Mom.

"Do you think Dad is looking for gold to...make money?" The possibility seemed ridiculous, and yet suddenly plausible.

"I doubt it," Grandma said, stepping forward. "Jack's never been interested in money. Never been able to hang onto it with his condition. And the way he looked at me the last time I saw him..." she shuddered. "Well, let's just say it wasn't greed I saw in his eyes."

"What does it matter?" Mom asked, exasperated. "Either way, he's not here." She folded her arms over her chest and leaned up against the wall of the cavern.

"You're tall." I looked over to see Cait had stepped forward and now stood before the man, who must have seemed like a giant to her. Her fingers played with the hair on one side of her head, long and straggly. "I like your braid. I wish I had a braid like that."

The man looked down at her, his face expressionless, as if he could care less about such things as braids and little girls. Though, of course, Cait was no ordinary little girl.

"Why don't you get your ma to braid your hair, then?" he asked. It was an innocent question, but we all stiffened. Cait looked down at her feet.

"She died," she said. Then looked back up at him. "Maybe you could do it for me."

It wasn't an outright request, exactly, but almost as if she were bargaining with him. He regarded her, but showed no sign of what he felt about the exchange.

"I got work to do, kid," he said, bringing his hammer back down to the ground and leaning on the thick wood handle.

She looked up at him, confused.

"Well, if you're looking for gold, why are you looking here?" she asked. "There isn't any in this wall." She gestured to the spot in the rock where he had obviously excavated. At the base of the wall stood a small pile of rocks, hammered out of the mountain by this enormous man before us.

The man turned to look at the wall, the divots made from his pickaxe cast into sharply contrasting shadows by his headlamp. Then he turned back, looked between Mom and Grandma, and then back down at Cait.

"Oh, yeah?" he asked. "Where would you look?"

Cait didn't hesitate.

"It's over there," she said, pointing her finger to a spot in the wall that sat untouched across the cavern lake.

The man blew out a breath, which might have been a snort of laughter if he hadn't been so stoic.

"Of course it is," he said, turning back to his pit in the floor. I couldn't imagine what he was doing inside it. I had always thought gold could simply be cut away from the rock it was found in.

"But it is," Cait insisted, looking back at us. "Aster, tell him."

I didn't know what to say. I took Mom's flashlight from her hands and shined it across the lake at the wall on the other side. I didn't see any hint of gold there. But I also didn't totally discount her proclamation. I turned back to her.

"How do you know?" I asked.

"Can't you see it?"

I shook my head.

She sighed, took the flashlight, and shined it onto a specific part of the wall.

"It's right there," she said, pointing again. Her finger made little swirls as she outlined what she must have thought was a vein of ore in the rock. Then, oddly, she stood there, almost as if in some sort of trance, her fingers making the same motion again and again.

I squinted, trying to see what she saw. But the only thing visible to me was the dirty brown rock that lined the rest of the cavern. No gold.

And yet I was intrigued. It had never occurred to me that Cait or Rhainn might have had powers of their own. Most people in the Fold were just ordinary folks as far as I knew. But maybe I had been wrong. Maybe little hints of magic were everywhere in the Triaden, and I had just been blind to them before now.

I stared around the cavern, searching, stupidly, for some sort of boat. I had never been a good swimmer, had, in fact, never gone into the water before that cold night I had spent on the sea, floating on a raft of Jade's rocks. And that time I had sunk like a stone before Erod had pulled me to the surface. There was no chance I could make it across this lake. I turned to Cait.

"Hey," I said. She ignored me, her fingers still swirling in the air. "Cait," I said, giving her shoulder a little shake. She shook her head, as if breaking a physical bond that had been holding her fast, and looked at me.

"Can you swim?"

She looked at me, raised her eyebrows and nodded.

"What?" Mom said, intervening. "No way. There is no way I'm about to let a little girl jump into a freezing lake in the middle of a mountain with nothing more than a gut feeling that she might find treasure on the other side."

Cait scowled, putting her hands on her hips in defiance.

"I can swim real good," she said. "Rhainn-y taught me when I was tiny. Besides, I know it's there. I can see things. The magic's in my blood. That's what Mama always said."

I looked back and forth between them. Two women, one mature, one small, were staring daggers at each other.

"Mom, I think we should take a look over there," I said, coming to Cait's defense.

She wheeled on me.

"What?"

"Just hear me out," I said. "Back in the Fold, there's magic everywhere. People can do things that wouldn't make sense to people on Earth. My best friend can move rocks with her mind." My heart gave a tight, miserable squeeze at the mention of Jade. She *had* been my best friend, at least. "I know someone else who can fly. Another who can brew potions to heal the sick. Me, for example." I looked down at Cait, who still wore her scowl. "I think we should at least take a look."

She glanced up at me, and when our eyes connected she understood that I was on her side. She moved to stand beside me, slipping her hand into mine.

"You really think you can swim all that way on your own?" I asked.

She looked out over the lake, sizing up the length from where we stood to the little beach on the other side, then nodded.

"Ugh!" Mom groaned.

She started kicking off her shoes.

"What are you doing?" I asked.

"I am not letting a little girl I barely know swim out into what could be a poisonous lake who-knows-how-deep to see if her x-ray gold vision is accurate."

"It's not poison." It was the man again. "I been drinking it for weeks. It's chock-full of minerals, but it won't kill you.

Mom glared at him.

"Give me that," she commanded, pointing to his pickaxe.

He looked over at the ax leaning up against the wall, considering for a moment. Then he nodded at Sean, who immediately went to retrieve the ax.

Mom stripped down to her underwear and t-shirt, picked up the ax and stepped over to the water. She put one toe tentatively into it and shivered.

"You owe me," she said, glaring at me.

I just shrugged.

Then, with one fluid movement, she stepped into the water and turned onto her back, holding the ax with both hands over her chest. She kicked off with her legs and began skimming across the surface towards the far wall.

"It's freezing!" she called when she was halfway. Her voice was intended to be angry, I was sure, but instead it had a sort of desperate sound to it, a surprise at the coldness of the water she couldn't mask with her irritation.

Finally, after what seemed like an hour, her head bumped gently against the rock on the other side. She flung the ax over her head, and it clattered onto the shore. Then, dragging herself out of the water, she lay facedown on the beach, her breath heaving.

But she must have been too cold to stay still for long. A moment later she was up on her feet, gripping the ax with an angry intensity.

"A little light, please!" she yelled from the other side.

We had all been standing, awestruck, watching. Now the flashlight and the man's headlamp shined across the cavern as we tried to light her way.

"Where is it?" she called.

"Over there!" Cait yelled. "To the left!"

Mom took a few steps to the side and raised the axe.

"No!" Cait called. "Lower!"

She readjusted her aim, and brought the ax down hard into the rock. Bits of dust and pebbles flew out with each thwack of the iron. I couldn't tell if she wanted to find the gold or prove me wrong, or just to warm her body with the effort, but she attacked that wall with a strength I didn't expect.

"Lower!" Cait called when Mom had yet to find anything.

I was glad to be on this side of the lake when the sound of her grumbling made it across the distance.

But then, suddenly, both her swings at the rock and her grumbling stopped. She knelt down, moving her head away so that more light could make it to the wall, and ran her hands along it in a similar swirling shape to what Cait had outlined in the air.

Then, she turned, and her voice was loud and surprised.

"I found it!" she yelled.

She turned back to the wall and continued to hack at it. Minutes passed, and soon the axe was dropped to her feet. She picked up a chunk of stone the size of a soccer ball and held it above her head, her face bright with triumph.

I looked down at Cait, who had her arms crossed, a happy smirk on her face.

"I tried to tell her," she said, shrugging.

I smiled down at her, and felt like a huge weight had been lifted. And in that moment I decided; I would still seek my father, try to bring him back to the Fold, try to save him. But with or without him, we now had a way to find the gold we needed.

# CHAPTER THIRTEEN

We arranged with the man, whose name turned out to be Carl, that we would work together to get the gold from the other side, then split the resulting riches. For a moment I considered whether this was a good idea or not. He seemed massive compared to the rest of us, and Sean was at least as big as Mom already. I guessed that they could probably defeat us all at once if it came down to a fight over the gold. But something in Carl's dark eyes calmed my fears. I trusted him. It was gut instinct.

He was quite a swimmer, himself, though he had let Mom be the one to take the initial risk. But his big size and strength meant that he could be the one to swim back and forth across the lake with the stones as she broke them free from the mountain. Within each, paper-thin veins of gold cut through the rock. He piled them one by one on our side of the shore, stopping to show me the pit he had dug into the rock where we had found him pounding the sledgehammer.

"You gotta grind it all up," he explained, showing me how to use the weight of the hammer to help put more force into bashing the rocks. "Then, you can fish the gold out."

He explained the basics of gold mining when done without the heavy machinery of modern times. First, the rock needed to be crushed into near dust. Then, using a pan and a bucket of water, one could gradually sift through the remaining tiny granules, the gold eventually settling onto the bottom and the rock particles floated out of the pan. It was intriguing to me that riches such as gold could be found amongst stones that showed little evidence of the gold within. But I balked at the weight of the sledgehammer.

"Can't you just melt it out or something?" I asked. I hadn't exactly been looking for such a physically demanding task.

"Nope," he said, turning to walk away.

And that was it.

I set to work, trying to attack my task with the same ferocity that Mom was bashing at that wall on the other side of the cavern. But after a half hour of pounding the sledgehammer into the ground, my fingers throbbed and my arms ached from the effort and the constant impact of the hammer against the rock.

Sean had set to work a few feet away from me, and I stood up now to see how our accomplishments stacked up against each other. There was no comparison. He had ground easily twice as much ore as I had in the same amount of time, and he had barely broken a sweat doing it. He smirked in my direction, an arrogant, superior air about him. I scowled.

I may have had an instinct to trust his father, but this kid was irritating. I silently hoped I didn't start to come off like him as I got older. It was annoying.

I couldn't imagine why anyone would go to such trouble for something like gold. That is, anyone except myself. In that moment, I felt I was the only one on Earth who had ever had a good reason for mining gold, and I couldn't think why anyone would be so brash as to wear an entire necklace of the stuff around her neck.

But I did have a good reason, and I had no choice but to continue my pounding. Across the pond, my mother hacked at the walls of the mountain like a madwoman, totally committed to my cause. And she wasn't complaining.

So I tried to keep my own complaints to myself.

Cait, being so little, busied herself with bringing me the rocks one by one as Carl delivered them. Then, while she waited for him to swim back and forth again, she would walk around the edge of the water, kicking pebbles and singing as she danced.

*"The child of Elyso looks at me*
*The child of Elyso sees my dreams..."*

I leaned back to watch her, wiping the sweat from my forehead with the front of my shirt. I was glad I was so fit from my months in the Fold. If this had been half a year ago, I would have given up by now. Cait didn't notice me looking at her, so I allowed myself to stare. Probably more than anyone else in this cavern, I had been amazed by her gold finding talent. Absently, I thought of Jade and how, in a different time, these two might have become good friends. Partners. Cait to find the gold, Jade to wield it.

I went back to my pounding, thinking of the rocks that built up the planets in the Triaden. Was this how those people had extracted the gold back there?

I turned back to Cait, suddenly curious.

"Hey, Cait," I called.

She turned at the sound of her name. I beckoned for her to come closer, but she only took a few tentative steps in my direction.

"How did you know there was gold in that wall?" I asked.

She huffed.

"I already told you, I could see—"

"I know, I know," I said. "But there isn't any gold on Aeso. Where did you learn to find it? I mean, if you've never seen gold before, how did you know what to look for?"

"I haven't practiced looking for gold before, silly," she said. "Of course not. I don't find gold. I find the wanted things."

"Wanted things?"

"Sure," she said, turning slightly to kick another rock into the water as she spoke, skipping a little as she did so. "Mama always said that was my special gift. A gift from the hills of Elyso. Once, when our dog Ginger had pups, one of them got lost down by the river. Ginger stayed back, had to tend the other pups, but Father wanted the lost one. He was worried about him. He took me with him to look, and I found him soon enough."

I sat back onto my heels, suddenly transfixed.

"Really?" I asked. "What else have you found?"

She twisted her mouth in an odd angle as she thought.

"Once, at the end of the growing season, I found a whole other field of apple trees nobody had seen before." Her eyes were wide as she told the tale, playing up the excitement of the event. "It was a good thing, too, cause Father told me that some in the village had nearly starved the year before. He told me that those trees would keep people alive who might have died from hunger."

Her face beamed with pride.

"And your Mama, she says the power comes from the hills?" I asked.

Cait nodded seriously.

"All kinds of magic waits in Elyso," she said, her voice hushed. "Mama said I was lucky I was born there. We don't have wizard kin. So that's where the magic had to come from."

"How do you do it?" I asked.

"I just see," she said, shrugging.

"What do you mean?" I asked. "What do you see?"

She furrowed her brows, clearly never having had this question posed to her before.

"Well, I see the person. I see what the person wants. They don't even need to tell me. Then, once I know it, I can just look for it for them. Things good people want sort of glow. And I follow the trail."

My mouth hung open as I tried to comprehend such a talent. And yet she seemed to have little idea of just how powerful an ability like this was.

She dropped her gaze, and then looked up at me, just briefly.

"That's how I knew about you," she said. She seemed to be still deciding if she believed her own words.

"You knew about me?" I asked.

"After the dream," she continued, "I didn't ever want to be near you again. But then I saw the glow in you. It's scary when there's no glow."

"You saw the glow in me, so you knew I was good?" I asked.

She nodded, her gaze on her feet, still kicking at the pebbles on the cavern floor.

Suddenly, my eyes stung, and for a moment I couldn't figure out why. Then I realized. Tears.

I stood up, almost walked over to hug her. But then I stopped, realizing my approach would probably frighten her. Even though she could *see* me, whatever horrors she had experienced in her dreams meant she still feared me.

"Can you see what I want?" I asked, my voice quiet.

She looked up.

"You want lots of things," she said.

I nodded.

"I can't see everything from home. We're too far away. But I can see the man. Your dad."

"You can see my dad?" I asked, shocked.

"Just since the night in that wrecked house," she said. "It's a little clearer now. I think we're going in the right direction."

Suddenly, it seemed, Cait had had enough. She skipped away, towards the other side of the shore, leaving me dumbstruck.

"Weird kid," Sean said. I hadn't noticed that his grinding had stopped along with my own.

I glared back at him.

"She's not weird," I said. "She found the gold, didn't she?"

He shrugged.

"Yeah, and *that's* weird." He turned back to his grinding, and soon was ignoring me again completely, his attention focused on his work.

Cait was right. I wanted a lot of things. But mostly the things I wanted didn't need searching for. There was no scavenger hunt that would work to bring Jade back from her insanity. No path Cait could take me along to force the Corentin to stop his torture of the people in the Fold and beyond.

But there was *one* thing I wanted that she could help me with. Now that we had gold, there was only one thing left on Earth that needed finding.

A smile cut through my tears and my awe as I realized the truth. In Cait, I had my own map, walking around within the mind of a five-year-old. If what she was saying was really true, and after the gold I was starting to believe her, she could direct us straight to whatever mountain hideaway my dad was holed up in. Sure, we might have found him without her help. But having her help would make everything so much easier.

I wondered if, like Brendan's power over the frame, and my power to run at great speed, her ability would fade as the days went on.

I turned back to my hole, taking up the sledgehammer with renewed vigor.

*Boom. Boom. Boom.*

It was only a matter of time now. Soon enough, we would have this gold. Then, we could move on, find Dad and the lost necklaces, and take both back to the Fold.

That had become my plan without my even realizing it. Finding the gold alone would not be enough, not for me, no matter how much ore we were able to dig out of this place. I was counting on the chance that bringing Dad back to the Fold with me could heal him. Just like it had healed me. Still, after more than half a year, I didn't have a good explanation as to why my health had suddenly turned. I could only attribute it to Kiron and the food he had given me that first night back in his cottage, his potions hidden within it. Though Larissa had laughed at that idea the moment it had been proposed.

Had it been something else, then? Another power, brought to life within me by my entering the Fold? I had met so many who carried such unusual gifts, people who had lived in the Fold since birth. It seemed there was something about that place, particularly the Triaden, that nurtured magical ability. Within the Fold was an energy that allowed, even encouraged, the extraordinary in its inhabitants.

It had taken me time to find my other powers. For months I had only despaired, convinced that the gifts of health and speed, while wonderful, would be the only benefits I would see from my time there. That I would be defeated in the end because I could not wield a force with enough strength to defeat a being like the Corentin.

But when I had unexpectedly found hope within me, the power passed down to me from Almara, himself, had finally flared. That hope, coupled with my hand against Owyn's old wood staff, had allowed me to escape the threat of death more than once since I had discovered it.

Could the same thing happen to my Dad? Could time spent in the Triaden bring him back to himself for good?

It was a risk. The madness of Almara, of Jade, were all encompassing, an evil so dark that it possessed their minds and shredded their dreams. I doubted any number of years in the Triaden could have helped them escape their dark visions, escape the Corentin. Would my dad heal, as I had? Or would he get worse, like Jade and Almara? All of us had the same blood in our veins. All of us faced the same foe.

It could go either way.

I sat back on my heels, leaning for a moment on the sledgehammer to rest. Cait flitted about the dark space, seemingly careless about yet another gloomy destination along this mad journey we were taking together. Her ability to keep her spirits lifted was incredible.

"Cait," I said. She hopped a few steps in my direction. "What do you see when someone's bad?"

She paused, a look coming over her face almost like she had been caught at something naughty.

"Nothing," she said, taking a step back from me.

"Nothing?" I asked. I was suddenly desperate to know.

"There's just…nothing," she said, turning to hop away again. "It's empty."

"What's so scary about that?" I asked, not necessarily meaning to speak the question aloud.

She looked back, her eyes at once fearful and reproachful. Then, as if the conversation had never happened at all, she turned and hopped away.

# CHAPTER FOURTEEN

Mom and Carl worked late into the night, stopping only to swim back across for dinner. Farther up the cave Grandma had lit a camp stove and was warming dinner rations over it in a small pot. The familiar smell of stew drifted over to me, and soon all of us were huddled around where she sat, stirring.

Grandma had spent the afternoon taking trips back and forth from the car, bringing supplies for the night down into the cave. Mom and Carl each had heavy blankets wrapped around them, warming them from the cold lake, and they held their hot tin bowls of stew close to their faces, eating greedily. When we were all fed, we sat staring at the lantern Grandma had placed in the center of our group, as if it were a campfire to warm us. Sean sat close to his father, and the two of them a little apart from the rest of us.

"Come here, girl," Carl said, gesturing to Cait.

She didn't hesitate, and it occurred to me that she must really like Carl, must see the good in him. She bounced over to him and sat down.

"Turn," he commanded, and she did. Then, with a skill I did not expect, he parted and smoothed out here hair and began braiding. Cait smiled.

"What's your story, Carl?" It was Grandma, who sat across the lantern from him, watching the two unlikely friends. "What's life like up in your village?"

"When things went south," he said, not looking up from his work, "we were already in a good spot. At least as far as the weather. We can grow some crops at that elevation, but not many. I don't like it down below, though."

"You got family, too. More than just Sean?" she asked.

He nodded.

"Yup. Another boy and a girl, not much older than this one." He nodded towards Cait.

"And a wife?"

His fingers paused, but only briefly.

"Ma's dead," Sean said. Then, as he felt his father stiffen beside him, "Sorry."

Carl looked down at his thick, worn hands, studying them.

"It's alright, son," he said. "We lost Gwen two winters back." His fingers stiffened with the statement, then he relaxed them and folded his hands.

Nobody spoke for a moment.

"I'm mighty sorry to hear that," Grandma finally said.

She sat quietly, then continued.

"How many are up in the mountains then?" she asked.

"In our village? Seventy three. There are two small towns, both to the north, but we don't see them often. Sometimes traders travel through. But getting around is difficult. Cars are scarce, and without a car, you can't get very far in the haze."

"How did you get down here?" I asked. I hadn't seen any other vehicle in front of the mine when we had arrived, and I couldn't imagine walking for long in the haze, especially up and down mountains.

"Hitched a ride with the supply truck," he said. He pulled a strip of leather from his pocket and broke it into a smaller piece for Cait's hair. "You ain't supposed to. The officials don't like to give rides to the locals. Say it wastes gas, gives the wrong impression. But I've known the drivers since I was your age. They looked the other way."

He completed the knot at the bottom of the braid, then gave the hair a gentle yank, telling Cait that his work was done. She had grown sleepy from the gentleness of his hands on her hair, and she crawled over to Mom and laid her head down in her lap.

"You need a ride back?" Mom asked.

Carl's face brightened.

"Yes, ma'am," he said. "I was already planning to head out in three days' time, when the trucks are supposed to come back through. But that's always a risk. That's why I've been away so long already. The last caravan wouldn't let me board." He scowled. "Animals. How anyone could leave a man in the haze when they have the means to help, I don't understand." Then, his face shifted, and his friendly smile returned. "A ride would be great, though."

He looked delighted about the whole situation. In the space of hours he had been reunited with his son, found a sizable amount of gold, and managed to avoid what I was sure would be a long and miserable trek through the mountains back home.

Mom turned to me.

"How much gold do you need?" she asked.

Over the course of the afternoon, I had managed to break apart enough rock to result in two walnut-sized piles of gold dust. It wasn't nearly enough.

"A lot more than this," I said.

She frowned, looking around the cavern.

"That's all there is here," came Cait's sleepy voice. I hadn't realized she was still awake and listening. Her eyes were closed.

Mom looked down at her, brushing her hand over her neatly plaited head.

"It's more than enough for me," Carl said, leaning back on his elbows. "What do you all need so much gold for?" The question was for all of us, but he was looking at me.

I shrugged.

"It's complicated," I said.

He laughed, leaning completely back and pulling the blanket up under his arms.

"It always is," he said.

"We'll have to look for more along the way, I guess," I said, turning to Mom.

She opened her mouth, as if to argue, but then stopped herself. Slowly, as we took step after step together along this journey, she was realizing that none of this was trivial. I hadn't concocted an adventure to find gold or find Dad. I hadn't made up the healthy heart beating in my chest. Cait hadn't accidentally found the vein of gold on the other side of the cavern. What was happening around her was real. It was a relief to see her finally start to believe.

"Okay," she said, and tried to give me a smile. Then, the exhaustion of first the poisoned haze and then the work in the mine caught up with her. She leaned back onto the rock, rolling onto her side, using her arm as a pillow.

Cait wiggled about as she found a spot beside her, dropping off to sleep almost instantly.

But as I, myself, lay back, and Grandma reached to click off the lantern, I saw that Mom's eyes were open and staring. I wondered how long it would take sleep to find her.

And me.

I couldn't be sure how long we slept. Not even a hint of sun could be seen from so deep within the mine. But some time later, the lights were on and the smell of food was once again floating in the air.

I rolled over, groaning at the aching in my arms and hands. It felt like they had been crushed by something very heavy, and I could barely wiggle my fingers.

Grandma had packed up most of our things, though had declined to haul it all back up out of the cave to the car. I was glad for the efforts she had gone to, though. I felt sure I could carry supplies out on my shoulders, just not in my hands.

Mom didn't seem to be doing much better than I was. She sat up from her spot on the rock and rubbed at her upper arms and shoulders, wincing as she did so.

Luckily for all of us, Carl seemed oblivious to any irritation from the previous day's efforts. Right after breakfast he and Sean both loaded up the majority of our things onto their backs and made it out to the car and back again in what seemed like no time at all.

"Wow," Carl said as he took the last steps from the tunnel into the cave when he returned. "You guys mean business; that car's stocked. Where you gonna head?"

I looked at Mom, then Grandma, and they both nodded.

"California, I guess," I said.

He gave me an appraising look, as if he was considering whether he should accompany us all the way. Then, as if remembering a bad dream, he shook off the temporary temptation.

"Well, I guess you'll be needing all you got, then," he said.

I wondered what image had flashed into his mind in that quick moment. And though I would be seeing the land between here and California myself very soon, I questioned him.

He walked over to his own pile of belongings and, after packing his tools and rough camp set into an enormous bag, slung the whole lot over his shoulder with a loud huff.

"You all ready?" he asked.

Everyone picked up the last of their belongings and followed him out of the cavern.

Carl took slow, deliberate steps up the incline towards the exit as he spoke.

"Out west," I said. "You said this is the edge now. What does that mean?"

"I could be wrong," he said, glancing at me. "I've only ever been maybe forty miles west of the mountains. But what I saw in that forty miles didn't make me think I'd find anything else if I went farther."

"What was it like?" I asked, adjusting the straps on my backpack.

"Desert," he said. "Nothing grows there at all anymore. The rains killed off the vegetation a long time ago, and when they finally stopped, what was left of the plant life never tried again. It's different in the east.

The water gets filtered as it sinks down into the dirt, and any seeds left below ground will sprout and grow, just like normal. At least until the rains come again and kill off the shoots."

"Yup," Grandma said, falling into step beside him. "I've seen it again and again on the farm. Stopped hoping a long time ago, though."

"Well, out west there's no sign of hope at all anymore," he said. "Not from what I've heard. Every ten years or so there'll be someone who wants to go west, scout it out, see if they can find better resources than what we've got up high. But every time, they either return with nothing, or don't return at all."

He glanced at me for a moment, and my heart fell into my stomach.

That could be me. Not returning. So far lost out in the middle of the wasteland that it would be suicide for anyone to even come looking.

"How do you grow crops so high up?" Grandma asked. "I still manage to farm enough for myself down below, covered with tents to protect from the rain. But I never knew you could grow in the mountains."

"Oh, sure," Carl said, adjusting the huge pack on his back. "We got good rain, just like everyone used to. Only problem is our growing season is so short. We start a lot inside, then move the seedlings out when the frost passes. Still, there've been years we've lost crops. The rain may be clean, but the weather's not as predictable as it used to be."

As we ascended the long tunnel, I could feel the air getting thicker, warmer. I pulled my face cloth over my nose and mouth, and paused to help Cait do the same. Carl didn't have a face cloth, and I doubt he would have accepted one if we had offered it.

Finally, we emerged into the light of day. He managed to shove his supplies between the barrels of gasoline and water, tightening them down with a thin rope that was dangling from the side of the trailer. Then, we all piled into the car, Cait sitting in the front seat in Carl's lap, and set off away from the mine.

To say the ride was uncomfortable would be an understatement. Carl's size, while impressive in the cavern, was unmanageable in the tiny sedan. Cait was cozy up front, but comfortable. The rest of us fought to share the little space that wasn't taken up by too many humans. The car groaned as Mom coerced it, weighted to the limit, up the dirt road.

I watched Cait as she eyeballed Carl's braid jealously, thicker and shinier than hers, as Mom turned back onto the highway. But then she quickly abandoned her stare to look out the window along the winding road. She wouldn't soon forget the feeling of carsickness that our journey had started with.

I was squished. I tried to keep my left arm and leg away from Sean, who sat in the middle, wanting to give him the space he needed to be comfortable. Not to mention that I hadn't counted on needing to snuggle up to anyone, especially some kid who seemed to loathe me. But my attempts were useless, and soon I resigned myself to the fact that we would be making this ride in very close quarters.

The car, now encumbered with the extra weight of Carl and his belongings, as well as the suddenly steep incline of the road, puttered along at a pace much slower than all of us would have liked. At one point, I felt certain that I could have outstripped it, myself, if I had had a bicycle to race against it. Still, it pushed on, slowly taking us up the steep mountainside.

Carl rested his head back, his face still unprotected, and closed his eyes.

"You all just keep on going," he said.

Carl dozed on. He looked like he hadn't slept for ages, and I guessed he was as relieved as we were to be on his way out of the haze.

In a way, we were lucky that the car was so slow. The road was slick, and if we had been able to travel faster, we probably would have met our death at the bottom of one of the steep cliffs we drove across. Someone had been through to plow, I could see, though not recently. Piles of snow lined the sides of the lanes, though several untouched inches of the stuff crunched beneath our tires.

We all fell silent as we took in the beauty. It was a relief to me. I had spent so long in the Fold, where the natural world was still healthy, that I hadn't realized how difficult these last days had been. Somehow, feeling my feet walk across ground that was vibrant and teeming with life helped ease the tension of the seriousness of my plight against the Corentin. But on Earth, where the ground was not only dead, but continually battered by rain after rain, my drive to continue on had been harder to maintain.

Now, I could see that there was something left worth fighting for *here* as well as in the Triaden.

Finally, Mom seemed unable to resist any longer. She stopped the car in the middle of a clear stretch of road and got out. Grandma laughed and quickly followed. I stared at them, surprised and a little worried at their sudden exit. But then I saw Mom, kneeling over with her hands outstretched towards the snow. The tips of her fingers brushed up against it, then made swirling motions through the thin drift she had found. She smiled, gripping a handful in her palm and standing up, staring at it as if it were the most precious, alien thing she had ever seen.

Cait popped open her door and jumped out, and while I was tempted to follow, I didn't.

Carl awoke at the gust of cold air from the open door, and leaned over to close it. Seeing the three of them, now frolicking in the snow like little girls, Sean nudged me with his elbow.

"Aren't you gonna go?" he asked.

My hand rested on the door handle, and for a moment I almost pulled it. But something stopped me.

"No," I said, releasing the handle and pressing my forehead against the glass.

I wanted to. A big part of me wanted to get out there, to forget everything that I was facing so that I could have a few moments of joy with my family. But the weight of my task was heavy in my chest, and it kept me inside the vehicle. I gritted my teeth, staring ahead.

"We need to get there," I said.

Carl turned back from the front seat, giving me an appraising look, and there must have been something about the look on my face that spoke to him. With a loud groan, he hauled himself out of the car, walked around and opened the driver's side door and slid into the seat. He punched his fist lightly against the horn in the steering wheel, and Mom, Grandma and Cait all looked up, surprised.

"Time to go, ladies," he called out the window as he rolled it down.

Their faces fell with the pronouncement. Then Mom took the opportunity to get one last fistful of snow and hauled it at the windshield, at Carl, where it splattered, melting a little in the morning sun.

They climbed into the car, their faces pink with the cold.

"Mind if I drive?" Carl asked Mom, who had taken the passenger seat, Cait tucking neatly into her lap.

"Not at all," she said, smiling back towards Grandma.

Cait was breathing in great gasps, a wide smile on her face, and Grandma rolled down her window. The air blew, gentle and biting at the same time, against her gray hair as Carl put the car into drive and hit the gas.

# CHAPTER FIFTEEN

It didn't take long to make it back to the village from there. As we rolled slowly into the tiny town, curious people stepped out from their houses to welcome Carl back home, wrapping scarves around their necks and pulling on their thick coats against the winter cold as they waved. Carl rolled down his window and nodded back at the familiar faces.

I was amazed as we moved deeper into the town. The little store from yesterday had been on the very outskirts, but as we penetrated beyond the outer houses, it was like driving through a history book written about a time I had never known. Dotted along the hillsides, little cabins spread out from the main road. Rooftops were covered in thick blankets of snow, smoke curling from nearly every chimney. Quaint. That was the word. The place seemed like the sort of destination a family might go to for a vacation back before the droughts began. Though now, vacations were mostly a thing of the past for the inhabitants of Earth. Looking around, I understood why Carl chose to remain here instead of down in the cities below. Here, the natural world was still free, still alive. To move to the city from a place like this would be like surrendering your freedom in exchange for a jail cell. Seeing this and remembering the city, my home reminded me of nothing more than a fortress designed to keep you alive. Functional, but without inspiration or joy.

Here, the joy shined from nearly every face. Their son had returned.

Carl turned the car up a side road, and the wheels spun against the icy pavement. But years of practice put his foot down hard on the gas, and we accelerated up the hill. He turned into a driveway, and before us a small cabin came into view.

A boy, maybe eight-years-old, opened the side door to the place and poked his head out. His face was suspicious, protective. Then from behind him, a younger girl, somewhere around Cait's age, burst through the door and ran towards the car.

"Daddy!" she shouted.

Her little feet scrambled atop the icy snow. Carl parked the car as the children slapped their hands against the driver's side window. He chuckled, opening the door.

They practically knocked him down into the snow with their hugs.

The rest of us stepped out of the car, and immediately the cold of the place took my breath away. It shouldn't have surprised me, with all the snow, but I immediately broke out into a wave of chills, shivering. The mine had been so warm, and even the stop Mom had made to inspect the snow had barely felt more than crisp as the air had come through the car window. But here the cold was biting. I grabbed the thin canvas jacket I'd brought and wrapped it around myself, though it did little good. My feet crunched along the ground as I came around the side of the car to meet Carl's family.

"Cathy, Dana, Aster, Cait," Carl said, pointing to each of us in turn. Then, "This is Caleb and Lily." He pointed to each of his children, ruffling each of their tousled heads of hair as he spoke their names. All of us nodded our heads in greeting. I crossed my arms over my chest, trying to keep the heat from leaching out of my body.

I felt awake. Maybe it was just that I was recovering from the effects of the haze, but the combination of the cold air, the snow and the vibrant faces were a new experience. I was suddenly excited to explore this strange place, where life went on almost as if nothing horrible had ever happened to Earth.

And it wasn't just me. All of us were smiling as we looked around, shivering in the frigid afternoon.

"Hey, old man." The voice was gruff and scratchy, and we turned to find a man dressed head to foot in animal skins stalking towards us through the snow.

It was the man from the store.

Carl's face, if it were possible, smiled even wider than before.

"Amos!" he shouted.

He broke apart from his children and went to greet the man, the two hugging each other like brothers.

As we stood, waiting to see what would happen next, I noticed Cait and Lily looking at each other, tentative smiles playing on their faces. I wondered when the last time was the Cait had seen another child her age, and I suspected a quick friendship was about to be made.

Caleb was staring at me, starting to hop up and down as the cold bit through his t-shirt and jeans. His look reminded me of a puppy getting ready to break out into a game of spontaneous chase with an older dog. Eager. Excited. I didn't know how to react to him, and I glanced nervously between him and his stoic older brother. My life had always been that of a reject. The other kids at school in the city had mostly ignored me. And in the Triaden there wasn't time for connections to be made with other children unless our lives depended on it. I found myself at once shy of Caleb and wary of Sean, suddenly unsure of how to behave around these people.

I looked up at the trees, the sunlight shining through the boughs that broke it into a thousand rays of light. Here, there was no need to form alliances based on the Corentin's actions, no worry about unlocking magical powers to ensure my survival. No monsters possessed the people. And the scenery was that of a beautiful, natural world, not that of the wasteland that was my home. I felt both comforted by the normalcy and concerned by it.

Finally, Carl and the man named Amos approached us. Lily raced to her father's side, and he picked her up and hugged her to him. She tucked her arms between her chest and his, trying to suck the warmth from his body.

"Glad to see you all found each other," Amos said. "We were starting to wonder when Carl would be making it back to us."

"Well, we have you to thank," Mom said.

"You didn't find the hermit then?" he asked. "This Jack you were looking for?"

Mom shook her head. "We have some ideas, though," she said.

"I heard," Amos said. "California, eh?" He shook his head. "If you're looking to kill yourself, I could just show you the highest cliff to jump off of around here." His eyes smiled despite the pronouncement.

Mom laughed.

"Let's go in," Carl said, and turned. His boots quickly collected the snow in the treads, making enormous footprints in the snow for us to follow. A giggle escaped Lily, and I realized Carl was tickling her sides as he approached the home he hadn't seen in many weeks. The sound of the little girl's laugh was easy, familiar. Noticing Cait watching Lily with a look like jealousy, I took her hand and smiled, suddenly feeling that everything was going to be okay. We all followed, and I for one was relieved at the prospect of warmth after just a few minutes standing out in the cold.

The inside of the cabin was smaller than it seemed from the outside, but it was cozy and warm, and I felt relief flood through me as the blood flow returned to my arms and legs. The walls were made of solid wood, animal skins draped across them. Looking around, I wondered where they all slept. Then, as I stepped further into the space, I realized a sleeping loft was built into the ceiling over the kitchen. The smell of cooking food was in the air, and on the small counter space a few empty packets of rations sat beside a small pot on the single-burner stove.

Carl slid Lily down and out of his arms. Sean immediately went to the cupboard and brought out a few more packets of food for the rest of us. Looking over his shoulder, I saw that the cupboard was nearly bare. His eyes caught mine as he turned back to the stove, and they narrowed as he shut the cabinet door with a snap.

*Pride.*

I watched him empty the contents of the packages into the already simmering pot, feeling guilty that we were here and seemingly about to take what looked like some of the last of their food. But once the food was in, he picked up the pile of discarded wrappers and stuffed the in the garbage can, then turned and blocked my view of the stove with his arms crossed.

*Geez.*

Carl meandered over to the ancient looking couch, and both it and he groaned as he lowered himself into it. Immediately, both Caleb and Lily were on top of him.

"What did you bring us?" they asked. Caleb was finally unable to contain himself further, and bounced on the couch next to his father.

"Daddy, where have you been?" Lily complained. "You've been gone so long. Look, I lost two teeth since I saw you last. *Two!*" She lifted her lips so he could inspect her teeth, giving her the comical appearance of a snarling beast.

"I know," Carl said. "I saw." He took one finger and slid it along the bottom edge of her lip, inspecting the now-vacant space in her mouth as if nothing more important in the world needed doing at that moment. Then, taking his hand away, his eyes widened. "You look like you got hit with one of Caleb's baseballs!"

She giggled.

"Caleb," he went on, "have you been hitting your sister in the face with baseballs again?"

"No!" he yelped, just slightly unsure whether or not his father was joking with him.

Carl smiled.

"But she hit me with a tree branch the other day," he said. "Look."

He smoothed back his black hair from his forehead, revealing a gash there that was well on its way to healing.

"Did you have it coming?" Carl asked.

"No!" Caleb answered.

"Yes!" Lily protested.

"Yes," Sean settled.

"Ah," Carl said. "Well then, perhaps you shouldn't underestimate your wee sister, eh?"

Caleb grimaced, but a moment later Carl's hands had found the boy's underarms and were tickling him ruthlessly. Caleb cackled with laughter, and the sound was so infectious that even Sean let a few chuckles loose from his tight chest.

Amos was fishing through a different cupboard, and soon he had passed all of us tea in mismatched cups. The tea was strange, sickly sweet and piping hot. I didn't care for the taste, but the warmth of the cup and of the liquid sliding down my throat was soothing. Soon we were all settled into the little room, our hands wrapped around our mugs.

"So, where you been, Carl?" Amos asked, settling himself on a cushion in front of the fire. "We were expecting you back weeks ago."

A shadow passed across Carl's face.

"I been in the same place the whole time," he said. "Delivery truck refused to give me a ride up the mountain. Nothing I could do but stay put and hope my luck would change. And it did." He nodded in our direction, and then pulled out the tiny plastic bag with his share of the gold floating inside it.

"Whoa!" Caleb said, making to snatch the bag away.

Carl was too quick for him, but it was clear that his father's haul was far greater than the children were used to. He held the bag up to the light for all to see. Just two bare lightbulbs hanging from wires lit the entire space, but the gold dust sparkled brilliantly as he tilted the bag, inspecting his pay for weeks of work, weeks away from his family. The looks on every face, including Amos', were like children gazing at a fireworks show. Amazed. Unbelieving.

Amos recovered first, cutting through the shocked silence.

"Good thing," he said. "Those same boys told us that after this trip, they won't be coming anymore."

Carl's hand dropped back to his side.

"What?"

His face instantly fell into a scowl, the same look he had had when explaining their refusal to take him up the mountain. But then, an unmistakable look of fear flashed across his face, and he rose from the couch, agitated. Even the children quieted at the change in his demeanor. He let out a long, slow breath, and I got the impression he was curbing a curse for the sake of the kids. He lumbered into the tiny kitchen space, leaning his hands against the counter, staring down at the floor as if the answers to how he was going to feed his family was a code hidden within the tiles.

All the life of the reunification party drained away. The children alternated staring blankly into space and then up at their father, trying to determine what this all meant for them.

"It'll be alright" Amos said. He stood up, too, and slapped Carl on the back with one hand. "We got crops."

"Not enough crops," Carl said, his voice quiet, his eyes still on the floor.

"Between what we got and the wildlife comin' back these days, we'll be okay," Amos said. "Besides, that's no small bag of gold you got there. That'll keep you all fed for a year or more."

"And what about everybody else?" Carl asked. "What about Martha and the girls? Or Mr. Jamison and the kids down at the school? Who's gonna feed them for a year or more?"

"We'll figure something out," Amos said. But the look on his face told the truth. It was clear he had been chewing on this problem for some time. And that he didn't have an answer.

Sean recovered before the other children.

"It'll be okay, Dad," he said, coming around to catch his father's eye.

"I bagged two deer last month alone."

Carl looked up.

"Two deer ain't gonna feed seventy three people, Sean," he said.

"No, but all of it together will," he argued. "If you found all that gold in just a few months, you can go get more. Can't you?"

Now Carl's gaze fell on Cait, and I knew that he was weighing the possibility of following us to California again. Following us into what he clearly thought was a suicide mission. I, for one, wouldn't have turned him down if he had really wanted to come. I knew that whatever he had seen the last time he had strayed from the mountains was terrifying to him. It seemed like the more help we had in a situation like that, the better off we'd be.

"There's always the city," Mom said.

It was an innocent comment, and she only meant to help, I was sure. But it was immediately clear that she had said the wrong thing.

"We ain't moving to the city," Carl boomed, rounding on her.

She had touched some sort of nerve. His voice was angry, and suddenly he seemed much larger than he had before.

Mom shrank back into the corner of the room where she had been leaning. In her surprise, she dropped her tea, the mug making a dull thunk as it hit the carpeted floor.

It occurred to me just how large Carl was. I wasn't sure if I should get to my feet, if I needed to defend my mother somehow, or if he was just blowing off steam. For a moment I neither sat nor stood, trying to decide. Amos saved me, stepping in front of him and putting one hand on his chest.

"That'll be enough, Carl," he said. "The woman is only trying—"

"Get your hands off me," Carl snapped, focusing his attention on

Amos now. His temper was rising with alarming speed. He pushed Amos' hand away angrily and shoved him backwards.

This was a mistake.

Amos came at Carl like a freight train, and I was surprised and not a little alarmed at the strength with which he pushed him up against his own kitchen cabinets.

"Knock it off, you idiot," Amos snarled, a fistful of Carls's shirt in his grip.

Carl's nostrils flared, and his chest heaved as he fought against Amos' hold. But there was nothing he could do. I couldn't tell how, but somehow Amos had him under control, even though Carl seemed twice his size.

A moment later Amos released him, his face disgusted.

Carl crumpled, sliding down to the ground. He sat against the cabinets and stared into space, his brief loss of control seemingly over. I stood back, staring between the two, amazed at the power the smaller man seemed to have over the larger.

I needed this Amos guy to give me some lessons.

Immediately, Carl's children were upon him again, this time hugging him to console.

"It'll be okay, Daddy," Lily said, wrapping her little arms around his thick neck.

Her voice in his ear seemed to bring him to his senses, and he patted her arm and kissed her cheek. A moment later, he unhooked her arms and smiled at her. Then, he climbed back to his feet.

"We've got a lot of work to do if we plan on staying here," he said, trying hard to smile at Sean.

The boy stepped forward as if he had just been called to duty. Sean was no longer a kid, that much was sure. He spoke and was spoken to like a man. One who deserved respect. One who had earned his place.

"Like I said," Sean said. "We're on our way. I've only gone maybe ten miles from here when I hunt, and only north. There's plenty more land to explore."

Carl nodded, then turned to Mom, who had just barely recovered from the unexpected outburst.

"I'm awfully sorry, Dana," he said.

He approached her slowly, like a hunter not wanting to frighten away his prey. He held out one hand to shake hers.

But Mom was having none of it. She crossed both arms over her chest, her tea forgotten on the floor where it had fallen. He had lost whatever trust she had had in him.

Realizing this, Carl dropped his eyes and turned back to Sean and Amos.

"Well, we better get to it," he said.

"Aww, Dad," Lily and Caleb complained at once. "But you just got back!"

"Yeah," he said. "And back I'll stay." He ran one hand lovingly down each of their cheeks and then turned to go.

I then realized something as he walked out the door that I hadn't really considered before. We really didn't know Carl at all. I didn't get the impression he was a bad guy. It seemed like he was just a man put under too much pressure for too long. But his outburst was a reminder that I didn't know what to expect of any one of the people accompanying me when they were put under pressure. How would Grandma react? Mom? Would they crack when faced with seemingly impossible tasks? Or would they rise up and take it all in stride?

I guess it didn't really matter. Who was I to judge my travel mates? I was the one hunting down a known madman to take along with the group.

But I couldn't help but remember Kiron's warning he had spoken to me so long ago, it felt like a different lifetime.

*Trust no one.*

# CHAPTER SIXTEEN

"Don't judge him too harshly," Grandma said ten minutes later. Carl, Amos and Sean had cleared out moments before, on their way to start their preparations for this new, unsupported life they intended to lead in the mountains. "The whole situation effects everyone differently. Some handle it better than others. But then, some have lost more than others, too." She glanced over at the small, framed picture sitting on the bookshelf. A woman, dark haired and pretty, stared back from the tiny portrait. "We're all doing the best we can."

Mom was staring out the window after them. Her fingers drummed on the windowsill, her teeth chewing on her bottom lip. Finally, when it seemed she was satisfied that they were truly gone, she turned.

"We're leaving," she said. "Now."

"But we just got here," Cait whined. She and Lily had found a spot on the floor to sit together, three dolls between them.

Caleb looked up from where he stood over the stove, stirring the pot as if feeding family and guests was something kids his age were expected to do every day.

"Where are you going?" he said. "Lunch is almost ready."

"I'm sorry, hon," Mom said, brushing past him. "But we've gotta get moving."

He tapped the spoon and set it on the counter, approaching her. He seemed concerned.

"Why? Cause of Dad? Don't worry about him."

Mom ignored him and cracked open the front door, pulling up the collar of her coat to cover her exposed neck.

"Let's go," she said. "You, too, Cait."

Cait made a frustrated sound, then threw down the doll she had been playing with and stomped across the room. I exchanged a glance with Grandma, but it was clear she was also in favor of leaving. Or, at least, not opposed to it. I was the last one out the door and I paused, turning to say goodbye to the two kids, left alone again. Looking around at the tiny cabin, I realized that there was a part of the warmth of the place that was just a facade. The walls had cracks that ran from floor to ceiling. The faint smell of mold hung in the air, though mostly overpowered by the smell of lunch. And Lily and Caleb, while friendly and smiling, were thin. Not starving, but thin. We were all just hanging onto whatever we could, doing whatever it took to survive.

"Well," I finally said. "See ya."

I turned and followed the other three back out towards the car, leaving Caleb staring as he stood in the doorway.

Mom was already in the driver's seat, fumbling with her seatbelt. I was sure that, if she hadn't been worried about calling attention to the fact that we were leaving, she would have honked the horn at me to tell me to hurry up. Once her belt was fastened, she settled for a familiar glare in my direction, and I shut the door behind me and made my way back out across the icy driveway.

Just as I was sliding into my seat beside a very put-out Cait, Mom put the key in the ignition. The engine turned over. And over. She paused, then tried again. The noise of the car trying to start continued, but no spark came to bring it back to life. She stopped again, staring at Grandma. There was no mistaking it; Grandma looked as worried as Mom did in that moment. We had told the kids we were leaving, and now we couldn't. My stomach swirled as I tried to think of what we'd do now.

What if we couldn't get the car to start?

How would we get to Dad then?

I fingered the familiar stone link around my neck, trying to imagine jumping with three other people all the way from here to California. It sounded miserable. In fact, making the number of jumps I would need to get all the way there would have been miserable on my own. With four of us it would be a nightmare.

Finally, after one last try, Mom seemed to give up, resting her forehead against the steering wheel.

Cait's breath came out in white clouds in the backseat of the car. I shoved my fingers, quickly freezing, between my thighs to keep them warm.

"What do we do now?" I asked, as much to myself as to Mom.

"I'll have a look," Grandma said, opening her door and hoisting herself out.

Mom pulled on the latch to unlock the hood, and Grandma propped it up with the precision of an expert. I guess year after year on the farm alone had taught her to be more self-sufficient than the rest of us. Though maybe that had always been the case. In the city, even before the drought, people didn't need to think about things like fixing cars on their own. They just called up the shop and men would come to tow the offending vehicle away, either repairing it or replacing it with something new. There had never been much need within those walls for that sort of resourcefulness.

But out in the rolling fields, where heavy traffic was now considered a single truck on any given day, resourcefulness was life. When the drought came, Grandma had erected two dozen growing beds in the sunny spot beside her house, where she could carefully control how much water each plant was given. When the rains came, she soon covered her precious vegetables with plastic sheeting to protect them from this new, most unexpected danger. And when the clean water in the pipes had run out, she had taught herself to distill her own drinking water from the acid runoff on the roof of the house.

She was not to be trifled with.

I caught glimpses of her from the crack beneath the hood. Her face was stern, concentrating.

"Try it again, Dana," she called.

Mom turned the key. The sound of the engine trying to come to life first caused excitement, and then, when it failed again, rattled me.

Through the crack, I saw Grandma rest both hands on the car, staring down at the engine as she tried to figure out the problem. I opened my door and hopped out to see if I could help.

I walked around the front, and she glanced up. The look on her face did not comfort me.

"Fuel pump," she muttered, staring back down.

"Oh," I said. "Is that bad?"

She snorted, then turned and rested against the car.

"Yep," she said, blowing a long sigh. "That's bad."

Mom's car door opened, and she walked around the front of the car.

From inside, I could hear Cait whining again.

"How bad is it?" Mom asked.

"Well, if there's an auto parts store around here, then we'll be able to make do," Grandma said. "Did you happen to see one on the drive up?"

We all fell silent.

"Maybe Carl has one," I suggested.

Mom shot me a look, but she knew as well as I did that we were going to need the man's help again before this was over.

"Yeah," Grandma said.

Hearing Cait's indignant complaints, I walked around to her side and opened her door.

"Go on back in," I said. "The car's broken."

Her protestations died on her lips.

"Yay!" she said, too excited to see her new friend again so soon to worry about how we were going to get anywhere now. She scrambled back towards the front door, opening it without bothering to knock, and not bothering to close it properly as she bounded inside.

"Lily!" she called, quickly disappearing back into the tiny cabin.

I turned back to the engine, nothing more to me than a snarl of hoses and wires and plugs I didn't understand. Grandma released the hood and let it fall closed with a slam.

How *were* we going to get anywhere now?

I shoved my hands into my armpits to warm them, but shivers were breaking out all over every inch of my exposed skin.

"Come on," I said. "Let's go back in before we freeze."

I walked back towards the cabin, but Mom and Grandma stood out in the cold for a few minutes longer. As I closed myself back into the warmth, I watched them talking out front.

"Don't worry," Caleb said from behind me. He reached around and held out a bowl of soup. "Dad's a whiz with cars. He'll be able to help."

A heavy knot of guilt hung in my chest. Here we had been about to abandon Carl, not even bothering to say goodbye, and now we would need his help to even make it out of the mountains. I looked up at Caleb, wondering how discreet he might be about our attempt at an early departure.

"It's okay," he said, still holding out the bowl. "I won't tell him."

In that moment I was more than grateful for Caleb's interest in me. An hour ago he had been annoying, but his desire to show his worth to the older kids was sure coming in handy now. It wasn't just that, though. Not only was he agreeing to keep our secret, but it had been his own idea to not tell Carl in the first place. It occurred to me that these people were used to making their own difficult decisions, even at a young age. They needed to be able to choose their own path in every circumstance, even dangerous ones. They needed to navigate each different personality of their neighbors, always keeping in mind the need to survive, always calculating how best to keep the peace while keeping themselves safe and fed. Even the kids.

I took the bowl of soup.

"Thanks," I said.

The bowl was hot, and it burned against my frozen fingers as I held it. I put it down on the counter and kept my fingers just an inch from the surface, soaking up the heat without searing my skin.

"Dad's not bad, you know," he said between blowing on the soup in his spoon. "He's just got a lot to deal with."

"I know," I said. I didn't, of course, but it seemed like the polite thing to say. The truth was, aside from the one outburst, being around

Carl had been easy. Downright pleasurable, even.

He glanced up at me again as he slurped his soup.

"Where are you guys going, anyways?" he asked, clearly trying to keep his tone casual. I wondered how happy he was living up here in the mountains, knowing that the world down below was unpleasant and threatening, but that the food always showed up with a consistency that could be counted on.

"California," I said, taking a bite of my own lunch.

"Whoa," he said, his spoon clinking back down into his bowl. "Why would you go to California?"

"My Dad is there," I said.

"Oh." Another bite of soup. "Are you going to live with him?"

I laughed, which surprised me considering what a mess we were in.

"No," I said. "We're going to get him. To bring him…home."

The front door opened, a waft of freezing air blowing through the cabin, sucking the heat through the doorway like a giant vacuum. Grandma rubbed her hands together and blew on them. She looked frozen solid.

"So," she said to Caleb. "Think you might have room for us for a bit longer?"

He smiled.

"Yup."

"Good boy," she said, nodding and smiling approvingly.

Mom looked on the verge of tears. I knew she was upset that we needed to stay. But I didn't understand why one single outburst from Carl had sent her into such a frenzy to get away. I, for one, was a lot more worried about getting the car fixed than having to deal with Carl's temper.

The girls had climbed to the sleeping loft while Caleb and I talked, and their giggles filled in the quiet spaces of our conversation.

"Caleb was telling me that his dad is good with cars," I said to Grandma. "He should be able to help us."

"Well, that's nice and all," she said. "But it doesn't matter how good he is with cars if he doesn't have the right part. Where do you think he and Sean and Amos ran off to, eh?"

"Oh, they're at Amos'," Caleb said. "He's the one who's sort of…in charge around here. His place has a big basement, full of maps and plans and stuff. They're probably looking at the growing maps. That's where Sean's been spending his days lately. Since we heard."

"How long do you expect they'll be?" Grandma asked.

"Probably a while," he said.

She slumped down onto the couch, hoisting her feet up on the wood chest that doubled as a coffee table.

"Well, I don't know about you all, but I don't have any desire to head out into that cold again until we have to. When Carl comes back, we can start the search for a new pump."

Mom slid into one of the four small chairs that surrounded the round dining table. Caleb looked back and forth between us and, finishing his soup, grabbed for one of the heavy winter coats hanging by the door.

"I think I'll go get him for you," he said.

"No, hon," Mom said. "They just left. Let them do what they need to."

"It's alright," he said. "I haven't been out yet today. Can you watch Lily, though?"

Mom smiled.

"Of course," she said. Her finger traced around the rim of the soup bowl Caleb had placed on the table for her.

I stood up.

"I think I'll go, too," I said.

Mom's eyes widened. It was one thing to let Caleb go out into the strange mountain town he called home. But for me to leave her when she was feeling so vulnerable seemed too much for her.

"It's okay," I said, trying to soothe her concerns. "I want to have a look around."

I nodded my head towards Caleb, trying to tell her without talking that it would be better if I could make sure he didn't say anything to Carl. He had said he wouldn't, but now that the car was dead we were in a fix. The last thing we needed was our host to change his mind about our staying in his house.

"You have a jacket I can wear?" I asked. "I didn't bring one." I pointed to my long sleeved canvas shirt. It was the warmest piece of clothing I owned, and it didn't seem like a good idea to reveal that the thin blanket from Kiron's had the powers it hid.

"Yeah, sure!" Caleb said, reaching for another coat hanging by the door and holding it out to me. His face was bright, clearly excited that I had chosen to join him.

I took the coat from him, heavy canvas, but lined with furred animal skins. It had a musty smell about it, but not entirely unpleasant. I buttoned it and followed him out the door.

"Aster," Mom called after me. "Be careful, okay? No... disappearing."

I laughed.

"No disappearing," I echoed.

# CHAPTER SEVENTEEN

We walked for a few minutes in silence, and I noticed that the weather was downright pleasant now that I was well insulated. I breathed deeply, and the smell of trees and snow were invigorating.

"How far is Amos'?" I asked after a few minutes. It seemed Caleb was waiting for me to start up the conversation.

"Not far," he said. His stride bounced a little at being spoken to. "Maybe half a mile."

Away from the road like this, several more small dwellings came into view, each on large plots of land. Beside them, nearly every one had covered greenhouses. This confused me.

"Why do you have to cover your crops if the rain up here is clean?" I asked.

Caleb looked up, confused for a minute, then smiled.

"Oh, we don't need to protect them from the rain. We need to protect them from the frost."

"Oh!" I said, feeling stupid. "I didn't think about that. It doesn't snow out of the mountains. Not anymore."

"What's it like down there?" he asked, no longer able to contain his enthusiasm.

"Where, the city?"

"Yeah," he said. "I heard they have big buildings where they grow food. Is that true? How do they *do* that?"

I spent a few minutes explaining the growing towers to him and, when I was done, what a typical day in the city was like.

"Wow," he said, his eyes becoming distant as he imagined it. Maybe to him it sounded glamourous. Or, at least, safe.

But no twinges of homesickness came to me while I recounted the life I had once led. Not now that I had traveled like I had, seen the amazing things I never would have witnessed had I stayed home. Now, the city had become boring, an artificial thing, flat and lifeless. It wasn't enough, not for me. Now that I had felt inspiration, true inspiration, I knew it needed to come from the dirt, the wind, the water. Outside the concrete fortresses, danger and beauty and magic combined to create a life I wanted to live.

And there was something else. Even though we all lived so close to one another in the city, I still felt disconnected. And though my heart condition had prevented me from making much in the way of friends before now, I think I would have felt the same way even if I had had a big social circle. Somehow, out here I belonged.

"I'd much rather live in the mountains," I said, looking up at the trees towering above, their branches intertwined into a lattice of cover. I hadn't been anywhere in the Fold like this, and yet it reminded me of what it was like to walk across those distant planets. I'd take these trees over the city's towers any day.

Caleb looked around, a look of distaste on his face.

"Why?" he asked.

"Well, it's beautiful for one thing."

"It's boring is what it is," he said. "There's only a few kids in town, and none of them are my age. Are there lots of kids in the city? There must be."

"Yeah," I said. "But they're not the best. At least, not in my opinion." I shrugged.

"Well, at least you have food," he said, finally winning the argument.

"Yeah," I said. "I guess you're right."

But as we continued up the hill towards Amos' place, and a lake of what I guessed was crystal clear water came into view between the trees, I was still happy to be far from the safety and sustenance the city offered. I wondered, if I was ever able to complete this monumental task before me, if I would ever be able to return home to those streets, to that little apartment Mom and I shared amidst the thousands of others. And in that moment, I decided.

*No.*

Caleb opened the door to the house without bothering to knock.

"Dad!" he called out, stomping his feet to rid them of the snow sticking between the treads.

A muffled sound came from somewhere inside, but nobody appeared.

"Downstairs," Caleb said. "Told ya."

We walked across the main living space, and I could tell why this place was the hub of activity for the village. This single room was huge, nearly as big as Grandma's entire downstairs, and plastered to the wall were so many maps that the original wallpaper was almost entirely covered.

Sean's face appeared at the top of a staircase, and he scowled.

"What are you doing here?" he asked, clearly annoyed. "This isn't kids' stuff, you know."

"Shut up, Sean," Caleb said. "Their car broke down and they're gonna want to get out of town soon. We need Dad's help."

Sean shifted his suspicious gaze onto me, and I nodded.

"Grandma said something about a fuel pump," I said.

He huffed and then turned to head back down to the basement.

We followed, and as we descended into the space, what I saw took my breath away.

Plants. Everywhere, every inch of table space was covered with hundreds of tiny plants. It was almost like walking into a growing tower, only on a much, much smaller scale.

"What's up, Aster?" Carl asked, looking up from one of the tiny seedlings he had been inspecting.

"It's our car," I said. "It won't start." Then, unable to contain myself, "What *is* all this?"

Amos laughed.

"It's our insurance plan," he said, walking around from behind the table. "We grow the babies inside as long as we can until the frost is gone. Then we plant in the ground where they can get sun. The season's short, so every plant needs all the help it can get. In a couple months, you'll barely be able to walk two feet through here. We got kale, chard, beans, tomatoes."

Carl snorted.

"Tomatoes are a waste, and you know it," he said.

"Don't hurt no one to have three tiny tomato plants," he said. His lips smacked unconsciously.

I imagined what Kiron's face would have looked like, walking into a place like this. He spent his days on magic and defending Stonemore now, but I knew his heart was in the working of vines and sprouts and all things that grow. I made a mental note to tell him about it when I saw him again. Then, as my chest squeezed with worry over him and everyone else I had left behind, I forced my gaze up and away from the plants.

Carl wiped his hands on his jeans and walked around.

"What's the matter with the car?" he asked.

"Fuel pump," Sean said.

I shot him a look. Did he have to take away the opportunity for Caleb to be the one to tell his dad?

But Caleb was still full of pride at having brought me here. I hoped that extended to him keeping our secret, too.

"Hmm," Carl said, thinking. "I don't think we have anything we can use for that here. That's not good news."

"What do you mean?" I asked, suddenly worried. "You mean, you can't fix it?"

"Oh, I'll be able to fix it," he said. "But it'll take a while. We can try to put in an order with the deliveries to have them send one up, but it won't be cheap. Those buggers will want nearly all your gold to trek back up here with something like that. Don't worry, though," he said, seeing my expression. "I can rip it apart and try to mend it. Wouldn't be the first time."

My heart fell. Either way, that didn't sound like we would be on the road again anytime soon.

Carl turned to Amos.

"I think this'll have to wait," he said. "Not much we can do right now, anyways, except spread out the seeds and make sure people are planting as much as they can. Amos, can you start getting the word out?"

"Sure," Amos said, nodding. "But I could use a hand, if you have one to spare."

"I got two," Carl said. "Sean, you go with Amos."

Clearly, this was not what Sean wanted to hear, and part of me felt victorious that he had been assigned to, in his eyes, the less important task.

"We better get back," he said, putting his arm around Caleb's shoulder. Caleb beamed. "Gotta get these folks back on the road."

Relief flooded me, both at Caleb's silence about our attempted escape, and about Carl's willingness to put his own responsibilities to the village aside so he could help us.

As we walked back, Carl didn't ask me why we had been trying to start the car when we had clearly just arrived. His eyes were on the ground, watching his own boots crunch through the clean, white snow. I could tell he was relieved to be home and chewing on the problems the village now faced.

"Does everybody grow their own food here?" I asked.

"Just about," he said. "Mrs. Jensen is eighty-seven and in a wheelchair, so she just works with the seedlings. It's her way of giving back to the rest of us. Her place makes Amos' basement look downright lazy by comparison."

"Do you think you'll have enough?" I asked. "I mean, now that the trucks aren't coming anymore?"

"Too soon to tell," he said. His breath made giant plumes of steam in the cold mountain air. He gripped one hand on Caleb's shoulder, giving him a squeeze. "We'll know a lot more after summer comes and goes."

"What will you do?" I asked. "What if it's not enough?"

"Well, I expect some people might head down to the city if that happens," he said. He released his hand from Caleb's shoulder and gave him a hearty shove, knocking him partway into a bank of snow we were walking past. "But we'll hold out as long as we can."

Caleb recovered and fell into step beside his father again, his hair now half-white from the feather-light snowflakes that clung to the black strands.

"Dad," he said, and I could tell he was about to ask for something. His voice had a sort of begging quality to it before he had barely said a word. "Maybe I can go live with Aster."

"What?" I asked.

Carl laughed.

"Son, did you even have a conversation with Aster, or his *mother*, about this idea? Not to mention me."

Caleb shrugged.

"I'm having a conversation with you about it now," he said. "Aster doesn't like the city. Maybe we could trade."

I stood with my mouth agape, both annoyed and impressed by this kid's resolve.

But the funny thing was that, in that moment, I was tempted to take him up on it. These mountains were beautiful, more spectacular than anyplace I'd ever been on Earth. If I did return when all was said and done, I knew I would at least pay this place an extended visit.

Carl stopped walking and turned to his son.

"Listen, kiddo," he said, placing one hand on each of Caleb's shoulders. "We're not going to rough it out here forever. If the summer passes, and our plantings fail, we'll all have no choice but to go down to the city."

"You'll never go to the city, though," he said, his eyes on the ground. "You've always said that."

"I know what I've said," Carl said. "Staying on out here takes resolve, and my refusal to go has been one of the ways I stay focused on life *here*, not there." He held out his hands before Caleb, like two sides of an old fashioned balancing scale. "But if it comes down to my pride in one hand and my family's lives in the other, I'll be choosing this side." The hand representing family sunk down low.

Caleb sighed, and I could tell that even though this was the answer he had been seemingly hoping for, he was unsatisfied.

Carl laughed and, wrapping one arm around Caleb's shoulder, began to walk again. He turned to me.

"Caleb here would have us move now," he said. "But not so much for the reasons he wants me to think. He's dreamed of the cities since he was small." He shook his head, clearly not relating to his son's ambitions. "But he can wait." He turned back to Caleb. "Either we go cause we're hungry, or you go cause you're eighteen. Got it?" He squeezed him tight to his side, and then released him again, giving him another shove like before.

This time, Caleb caught himself before falling into the snow.

He stood up tall, his own expression of pride mirroring that of his father's. Then, despite his best attempts to remain stoic, his face broke into a wide smile.

Carl inspected the car when we got back to the cabin and proclaimed he would be able to repair it, but that it would take time. He estimated two days before he would be able to get the torch he needed from the other side of the village to work on the metal part of the pump, and then another day for the actual repair. And that was if things went according to plan. At first, I squirmed at the thought of such a delay. But as the sky clouded over late in the day and snowflakes began to fall, I decided that at least this was a pleasant place to be stranded. The peaceful feeling brought on by the snowfall was unexpected, and entirely welcome.

That night Grandma unloaded several days' worth of rations from the trailer to share with everyone. And as we finished up dinner, Mom had let most of her frostiness towards Carl thaw. Though it was clear she still didn't completely trust him. The two of them carefully avoided each other as the night wore on. Carl seemed to understand that nothing he could say could fix his behavior earlier in the day, and eventually he stopped trying to force his apologies on her.

When the lights finally went out for the evening, and we were all tucked in together on the living room floor, I scooted over to her.

"Why are you still so freaked out?" I asked, my voice barely audible as I spoke directly into her ear. "It's not like he attacked you or something. And he's fixing the car for us. What's the big deal?"

She sighed.

"It doesn't matter," she said. "Not to me. You don't understand. With your dad, it was always this way. One second he'd be hugging me, kissing me, and the next I'd be down on the floor. He would snap, just like that. It got to the point that I never knew what to expect, so I was just scared all the time." She was quiet for a moment. "All the time," she repeated.

I had seen Dad hit her once, but it had never occurred to me that it had happened more frequently than just the one time my four-year-old brain had hung onto.

"I don't think he's going to hit you—" I began.

"I know, I know," she said, cutting me off. "But once someone starts acting like that, doing unexpected things, *scary* things, it's hard to forget. Hard for me to, at least."

I sat in the quiet for a while, the only sound was the last of the fire crackling down to embers.

"I'm sorry that I'm making you see Dad again," I said finally. "I didn't know."

"Oh, don't worry about that," she said, her voice immediately sounded tougher, stronger, and I wondered if she, too, was remembering being knocked to the floor. And the strength it had taken her to pick herself up and move on without him in her life. "I know how to deal with your father. But when someone you don't expect, someone you trust, when they do something to hurt you, it's hard to go back."

So she didn't care about Carl's attempts at restitution. She felt she had seen the true man behind the quiet, kind exterior. And while I didn't agree, I understood.

Suddenly, the image of Jade standing over me as the Fire Mountains crumbled around us unwittingly flashed in my head. A crawling sensation crept over my skin, making me feel cold despite the warmth of the room. In my mind, I stared into those deep green eyes, watched them succumb to the black of the Corentin's possession. But the black of her eyes, the only visible sign of his possession of her, hadn't come until the very end, not until she was completely in his grasp. How long had she been doing his bidding before that day had finally come?

"I know someone like that, too," I whispered in the darkness. "I don't know what will happen if I ever see her again. I don't know if I can ever trust her again after what she did." My hand raised automatically to my forehead, right over the spot where she had struck me with the rock in her Riverstone chamber. I paused, listening to the last pops of the wood as it slowly turned to ash. "Do you think people can change? Do you think there's anything they can do to win that trust back?" I tried to imagine what Jade could possibly do to prove herself to me once more, to show that she had never meant any of it, that she would never break my trust again.

At this question, Mom was quiet for a long time, and I had started to wonder if she had fallen asleep. But then, just as my own mind started to wander as sleep overcame me, she whispered her answer into the dark warmth of the room, and it filled my veins with ice.

"No."

# CHAPTER EIGHTEEN

She was screaming.

Jade hung from the precipice, the same one within the Fire Mountains that she had left me dangling from at the moment she had lost all reason. I stood above her, watching her, her green eyes piercing my own as loudly as her screams pierced my eardrums.

"Aster!" she begged. "Help me!"

I felt frozen, unable to decide whether to trust her again.

*She only wants to save herself.*

I started to kneel down, to extend my hand, but the thought brought me up short.

*She'll kill you.*

One of her hands slipped off the rock, and suddenly she was dangling by just five fingertips, gripping onto the last piece of mountain before her strength gave out, before she would be sent careening to her death.

"Aster!" she screamed, her body flailing as it hung over the great chasm.

My body made the decision for me, and I dropped to the rock, flat against my stomach. I held out one hand, and in an instant, she gripped it with her free one. With strength I didn't know I possessed, I hauled her up the side of the rock. She held my arm with both hands now, and with one final lurch, I thrust her over the edge until she, too, rested on her stomach. We both lay, panting and sweating, catching our breath.

I sat up, staring down at her, the girl who had put me through so much. She had made me doubt myself. She had left me for dead, and when that didn't work, had attacked me outright. But the eyes that had looked up at me as she had dangled had been her own, not the Corentin's. She sat up, and I waited for her to thank me. I was eager to hear her words, to determine if I had made the right decision based on her response.

But words didn't come from her lips.

Only screams.

She backed up, scrambling away from me, staring wildly at me as if I were the devil, himself.

"Jade, what are you—" I began, but it was no use. Her wails of terror echoed against the cavern walls. From deep below, I heard her screams joined by those of dragons.

"Jade!" I hissed. "Stop screaming! They'll come!"

But she didn't stop. When her back finally hit the wall, and there was nowhere else for her to flee, she simply sat and stared as scream after scream ripped from her lips and, finally, ripped me from the dream.

I was on the floor of the cabin. I lurched to sitting, stared around in a panic.

*Just a dream.*

Then who was screaming now?

The sound didn't echo here, and instead was close to my head, so close that I clapped my hands over my ears and backed away, too distracted to even realize what was happening. But the early morning light was coming through the window, and I saw the face of the person making the sound. Saw the terror on her face.

It was Cait.

Relief flooded through me as I realized what was happening. Another dream.

"Cait, it's okay," I said, trying to reach out to her, to calm her.

She scrambled backwards, just as Jade had done in my dream only moments before.

"Cait, it's Aster," I said. "It was only a dream."

But that was the wrong thing to say. Confirming my name only increased her terror, and she screamed louder and louder as each second passed.

Mom was on her feet, blearily staring around the tiny room, trying to figure out what was happening. Seeing Cait, she lurched towards her, gripped her body in a tight hug, tried to rock her. Cait fought wildly at the restriction, arms and legs flailing, fingernails digging into Mom's forearm.

"Calm down!" I yelled, trying to match her energy. "Remember the glow!"

She turned away, her chin held against Mom's shoulder, still scrambling desperately to make her escape. I went around the other side and forced her to look into my face.

"I have the glow, Cait!" I yelled. "I can't be him if I have the glow!"

As the words came out, I suddenly understood that they were true. It wasn't me she was fleeing, it was the Corentin. Something about the dreams or visions she was having were confusing her, making her think that I had somehow become the monster she so feared.

Suddenly, at my voice, her thrashing stopped, and her eyes got a glazed sort of look in them. Mom still gripped onto her, but she now hung limply in her arms, her mouth slack. Then, a cloud of black mist began to threaten the corners of her eyes, bleeding into the whites like ink into water. I backed up, alarmed, as the same black irises I had seen in Jade, in Owyn, in the Coyle, began to dominate those of the little girl.

"You cannot run," she said quietly, her voice gravelly and decades older than her own.

"No," I said, barely able to breath. "No."

*NO NO NO.*

"Yes," she said.

Her lips slowly stretched into a sneer. As her body relaxed, Mom's hold did, too.

"Mom!" I yelped. "Don't let her go!"

But I was too late. Cait launched over Mom's shoulder and slammed into my chest. The force of her leap knocked me backwards, and I found myself on the floor with her straddling me, those too-familiar black irises staring down at me.

"He said I can't kill you," she said. "But I can. No man can stop me, no matter how old, no matter how burned, no matter how badly he wants to save his precious Fold."

I tried to sit up, but her little body was heavy against mine, holding me pinned to the ground as if she weighed a thousand pounds. My mind raced as I tried to put the pieces together, tried to understand what was happening. But she was too fast. *He* was too fast. Her hands fastened around my throat and squeezed with the strength of someone ten times my size. I gagged, and then all the air flow stopped, and nothing got in or out.

"Cait!" Mom screamed, suddenly realizing that I lacked the strength to throw her off me.

She stood up and grabbed her arms, tried to wrench her free. Cait fought, her black eyes glinting in the dim light, her mouth opening into a snarl as if she were readying herself to tear me to shreds with nothing but her teeth.

Mom seemed to understand the danger, seemed to register that the little girl was somehow hurting me, was somehow far more powerful in that instant than I was. Her face became wild, like an animal defending her cub, and with a force I did not expect she grabbed for Cait's arms again and ripped them away. I was certain in that instant that she was also alight with the glow of power that Cait was so used to seeing, though I saw nothing but the terrifying look on her face. She picked up Cait and threw her across the room, where she landed against the sofa. Mom turned in front of me and took a defensive stance, ready to fight.

But Cait crumpled, and when she looked up again she seemed confused, their original blue returning. As she came back to reality, she seemed to realize what had happened. Her face scrunched into a look of pain so intense that the howl that burst from her throat did not do it justice.

I scrambled to my feet, pushing past Mom's arms, still outstretched to protect me.

"It's okay," I said, both to Mom and to Cait.

I crossed the floor in three long strides, picked up the little girl and hugged her to me. I should have been terrified of her, but in that instant I was more worried about her than anything else in the world.

"It's okay," I said. "It's over now."

She didn't have the chance to fight me. Her body slumped into mine, exhausted and tortured, and I rocked her back and forth like I had seen Mom do days before.

"What is going on?" Mom yelled, unable to keep her voice calm.

Everyone else had awakened at the struggle, and five confused sets of eyes watched our exchange.

I held her tighter.

"He broke through," I said. I felt like I might pass out, the only thing keeping me conscious was the tormented little girl in my arms. "The Corentin. He possessed her."

*He can possess her.*

*From the other side of the cosmos.*

"It's okay," I said again. Rocking. Rocking.

But it wasn't okay. Something had changed. Or had it? Hadn't I suspected it, myself? Hadn't I thought that my own father had been possessed, just like Cait had been now? Wasn't I, in fact, hoping that that was the case? That there was hope in saving him?

I had thought that, did still think that. But I hadn't counted on him finding other ways to target me, other people to destroy along his path to destroying me.

I should have known. I remembered all those children, lined up in tidy rows in the Coyle's tent, their eyes blank and staring. I had hoped that, getting far away, Cait would be able to leave all that behind. That she could find peace here, even on this broken planet, far away from the one who had tormented her for so long.

As the truth came crashing down around me, I realized that no distance would make Cait safe. Or Dad. Or anyone. The Corentin wanted *me* now. He would not stop until, somehow, he had me either in his command or dead.

I looked around the room. Carl and his children were huddled together on the staircase, even the tall, powerful man fearful and confused.

Nobody was safe. He would strike again and again, as long as he could find me. His words, spoken through Cait, had been true; I couldn't run. Not for long, at least. He would find me and target whoever traveled in my company. He would take them all, one by one, until nobody remained to me but an army of people who had once been my friends and had fallen to the enemy in exchange for their allegiance.

Dad was already far gone, though whether possessed or truly mad, I didn't know. I did know that I had to find him, that I had to try to bring him back with me. There was a chance he could be healed, just as I had. Then, maybe together we could discover some way to defeat the monster that had caused all this destruction.

And he had the gold.

I hugged Cait tighter as I realized what I had to do.

I looked up into the face of my mother. It had only been days that we had been reunited. She wouldn't understand. But I couldn't stand it, couldn't watch her fall, too. If I allowed that to happen, I felt sure I would break into a thousand pieces. I had to keep her safe. And the only way I could think to do that was to get away.

When my eyes met Grandma's, though, I was surprised by what I saw there. A respect I had never seen before stared back at me. She looked at me like she understood my mind, though how I had no idea.

I released Cait, who slumped to the floor in a heap.

"We have to go," I said.

I stared around the room, began collecting my scant belongings and stuffing them into my bag. I took the water jug Grandma had brought in to share with Carl and packed it into the top section of the backpack, sliding the drawstring closure tight and tying it into a knot. I heaved the pack over my back and took a deep breath, staring at Mom.

"We can't go," she said. "He said three days. Don't you remember? It'll be three days at least."

"You don't understand," I said.

I walked to her and hugged her, tightening my arms around her middle, taking in one last breath of her before making my escape. A plan was forming in my mind, and I struggled to choke the words out before losing my nerve. I pulled away, unable to fight the tears running down my face.

"Go back to the farm," I said, coughing a little as my throat closed with the echo of pain on the spot where Cait's fingers had pressed. "When this is over, if I make it, I'll meet you back there. I don't know how long it will take."

"What are you talking about?" she asked. "I don't—"

"I know this seems crazy," I said. "But he's coming for you. The Corentin. He's already found Cait. It's only a matter of time before he gets to you."

"Now, you listen to me," she began, her face hardening as she started to understand my intention.

"No," I said. "He's coming for you. I have to go now. I would go alone, but I need Cait to help me find Dad."

"No," she said, shaking her head, trying to reach out to grab me. "No, you said we were going together. You said—"

"I know what I said."

Grandma stood up from the couch and walked to me, taking one of my hands in both of hers. Her eyes were sad, maybe sadder than Mom's, but no tears came.

"I was wrong," I continued. "If I don't go now, he'll take you all, one by one."

"I don't care," Mom said, her voice cracking. "I don't care if I die. I don't care if he takes over my mind or tortures me or cuts me up into little pieces. Aster—"

"I do," I said. "This is the only way. You have to trust me."

I walked back to Cait, wrapped the blanket she had slept beneath around her small, shaking body, and picked her up.

"Meet me at the farm," I repeated.

I moved to hug her, her eyes wide and staring as she struggled to comprehend what was about to happen. But I stopped short when I saw the one thing that could only confirm my worst fear. And the last thing I had ever wanted to see in my life.

Black wisps of smoke danced, almost playfully, in the corners of my mother's eyes.

I gulped, staring around the room, suddenly worried that any moment now every single person here would be within the Corentin's command. But every other set of eyes was clear. And when I turned back to her again, hers were, too.

Had I imagined it? Was my paranoia making me see things?

"I love you," I said, backing away. "I'll be back as soon as I can. I promise."

I headed for the door.

"Aster, wait!" Mom screamed. As the door slammed shut behind me, I could hear the commotion from behind it. She was trying to come after me. Grandma was holding her back.

I walked twenty feet away from the cabin through the thick blanket of snow, the bitter cold air stinging the skin on my cheeks as I came, exposed, into the morning. Cait was crying again, and her little voice making sad, hiccuping sounds as we walked away. I dug out the link from my pocket and stopped, staring down at it.

Maybe it was for the best. Maybe it wouldn't have even gotten all of us far enough if I had had the courage to use it for our entire party.

Just to check, just to be sure, I leaned back, forced Cait to lock her gaze with mine. Blue irises stared back.

"Do you trust me?" I asked. Then, when she didn't respond. "Do you see the glow?"

Her face seemed to clear, and the total misery that had been there a moment before flickered away. She did see it. Deep inside, she knew that what I was doing was right. That I was good.

She nodded.

The front door to the cabin burst open, and the sound of Mom struggling to get to me rang out through the morning. Was she trying to attack me? Or did she just want to keep me, her son, from abandoning her yet again?

But I didn't listen, tried to shut my ears to the wail of despair coming from her.

I faced west, lifted the link, gripped Cait tight, and jumped.

# CHAPTER NINETEEN

Five times. Ten. Twenty. I jumped again and again, Cait's little body bundled up against mine. I needed to put distance between us and what remained of my family. I shouted the link's command again and again.

*"Forasha!"*

*"Forasha!"*

*"Forasha!"*

It must have been hours, but I couldn't tell. Time blurred past me as I fled. With each landing, my hand automatically raised up into the air again, thrust us anew through the next portal. And the next. We slowly made our way across the mountain range. Snow, trees, lakes, rivers, all blew by us. We saw no other villages, no outposts where people were hiding out, making a go of life, alone and up high.

After a while, Cait's sobbing stopped. It was only when my legs could no longer support our weight, collapsing on dry, hot earth, that I finally fell to the ground, no longer able to sustain our flight.

Cait rolled away, lay lifeless in a heap against the rocky sand. We had finally left the mountains.

I was on my back, staring up into a gray sky, the tears long since having dried on my cheeks. The air moved, just barely, in and out of my lungs. The tightness of loss still hung heavy within every cell of my body.

Somewhere up there, beyond the blue-gray skies of Earth, across vast oceans of stars, the Corentin stared back, searching. I knew it. Could feel it. Could he see me now? Had we moved fast enough to lose him?

Finally, a whimpering sound came from the heavy blanket I had wrapped around Cait, and she emerged from the ball, her face bright red and miserable. She stared around the landscape, and whatever hope had remained in her eyes was washed away in an instant.

"Where are we?" came her tiny voice.

Wind whipped through her hair and over my skin. I blinked the brightness of the sunlight away, came back to myself.

I sat up and looked around. Behind us, the west side of the Rocky Mountains loomed, enormous and green. Before us, nothing but flat, barren earth. And in the distance, somewhere far away and out of sight, another set of mountains rose from the desert floor. Our destination.

I turned back to take in the range we had just tumbled out of. There, the last of Earth's treasures stood, still clinging to life miles up into the sky. There, somewhere within the endless folds of rock, was my mother. Left behind. Again.

Something about the thought, about imagining her anger, her fear, brought me back to myself. I could not despair. I hadn't made the choice to leave so that I could quit, shriveling up beneath the desert sun after barely having left.

"We're somewhere in Utah, I think," I said.

The words meant nothing to her. She stared around, her face despondent.

"You okay?" I asked.

Her breath caught in her chest, and little cries started coming from her. I crawled closer to her and gathered her into my arms, rocking her slightly as we caught our breath.

Had it been real? Had the black I had seen in my mother's eyes truly been the Corentin reaching out for her? Or had it just been a figment of my imagination, my fear making things up as we had fled?

I wanted to tell myself that it didn't matter, that if it had been real it had only proven that I had made the right decision to go when we did.

But it did matter. If he really had possessed her in that moment, would the Corentin release his hold on her and come looking for me? Or would he latch onto her mind and continue tormenting her for the fun of it?

More tears rolled hotly down my cheeks. Cait slowly calmed, and I was relieved to find her eyes still clear when she looked up at me again.

"What's happening?" she asked, fearful and shivering despite the heat of the sun.

I hugged her tighter, desperately wanting to protect her, but unable to decide if withholding the truth would do that, or somehow put her in greater peril.

"You know how you get when you find something you're looking for?" I asked. "When you find something using your power? How you sort of go into a trance?"

She stared at me, her face blank

"When it happens, it's almost like you're not really here, not entirely. Like sleepwalking."

She nodded, understanding.

"Rhainn-y used to sleepwalk," she said. Her voice caught at the memory of her brother.

"Well, you sort of get that way, when you've almost found something. Like when you found the gold in that mine. And that's what happened this morning. Only it was the Corentin doing it to you, not your power."

Her eyes grew wide with fear at the mention of the name.

"What do you mean?" she asked.

"It's like he's using you to talk to me," I said, trying hard to make the whole thing sound less scary than it was.

Her gaze shifted, and she stared into space for several long moments.

"How do I make it stop?" she finally asked.

"Stop?" I asked. "I don't know if you can." But then the thought occurred to me that maybe she could. If she couldn't halt the possession completely, I wondered if she could take some sort of control over it. "What does it feel like when it happens? Do you remember it?"

"I get sort of tired," she said. "Like the way it feels right before you fall asleep. It gets dark all around, and I want to lay down, but I don't because of the noise."

"The noise?"

"The scary man is always talking so much that I can't sleep," she said, furrowing her brow in irritation. "Even though I want to."

*The scary man.*

Was that what it felt like for Jade, too? For my father?

I turned her to face me.

"If it happens again, if you start to feel that sleepy feeling and the scary man it talking, can you try something for me?" I asked. She looked up tentatively, not ready to promise anything. "Try to stay awake. Try as hard as you can to stay awake. Can you do that?"

"I guess," she said, shrugging. "But what if I want to sleep?"

"You can sleep during normal times," I said. "But if you hear the scary man talking and you start to feel sleepy, I want you to try as hard as you can to stay awake. Okay?"

"Okay," she said.

I hugged her to me again, gripping tightly to the one person on this planet that I still had by my side. Even if part of the time she *was* the Corentin's puppet. It was a risk I had to take.

Maybe it was possible. Maybe she could fight it. Everyone I had ever seen possessed by the Corentin had always seemed too far gone to fight. But Cait still had her wits about her most of the time. Maybe, with a little help from me, she stood a chance against him. Maybe we both did.

I wished I had thought to tell Mom the same thing.

Finally, when we had held each other for many long minutes, she let the blankets fall away from her shoulders and stood up, stretching her arms high above her head.

Immediately, I wished to do the same. I had traveled like this, jump after jump, not long ago, but I had never been able to put my finger on just why it was so uncomfortable to do so. Cait groaned as her muscles stretched out, releasing the tension packed tight within them from the jumps.

I got to my feet and stretched my arms up, too. It seemed I could feel every fiber of muscle slowly releasing, and the relief was palpable. Immediately I felt better, more cheerful. Or at least, less weighted by my decision.

When we had both stretched out, we stood, staring around.

There was nothing here. Hot wind blew against our faces, unnatural for this time of year. I knew that, in another time, this place would have been vibrant and green. Or maybe even white with a dusting of snow. Now, there was nothing left. The rains had stopped coming decades ago. It was a wasteland.

"Wanna walk for a while?" I asked. I knew that the sun would grow hotter as the day dragged on, knew that we should get moving, but I couldn't bring myself to jump again quite yet.

Cait nodded, looking down at the blanket she had emerged from, a question on her face.

"Just leave it," I said. "We won't need it."

Kiron's blanket had been enough to keep me insulated in three feet of snow, had kept Cait safe beneath poisoned rain. I counted on it now to keep us warm if the heat in this stark desert suddenly disappeared.

We walked for a time in silence, relishing the feeling of no longer being constricted by the jumps. Cait skipped alongside me, occasionally kicking rocks that cropped up in her path. I was amazed by her lack of argument about our current situation. Not to mention the fact that she seemed to have gotten over her fear of me so quickly. I wondered if she was able to fight off the Corentin, she might fight off the memory of her dreams as well.

"What do you dream about?" I asked, kicking a rock, myself. "I mean, when you have your nightmares?" I remembered the dream I had been having about Jade screaming just before I had woken up to find it was Cait.

She didn't speak, and I noticed that her skipping walk and rock kicking ceased.

"Cait?" I pressed. "You should probably tell me. We're alone now, and I need to know what to do if it happens again." My hand lifted absently to my neck, still sore from where she had gripped her little hands around it.

Her gait slowed, and eventually she came to a stop. She looked around us, at the ground, at the mountains in the distance, at the sky. Anywhere but at me.

I knelt down, forcing her to meet my gaze.

"It's okay," I said. "Nothing's going to happen to you just for telling me."

Finally, she willingly looked into my eyes.

"You don't know that," she said.

I wondered what it was like for her, to be experiencing so much misery at such a young age.

She had been a favorite of the Coyle, if only because both myself and Rhainn had tried so desperately to free her from him. The fear she felt towards him still hovered over her.

And we both knew the truth. That neither of us understood for sure just how far the Corentin's actual powers could reach.

Finally, she made her decision. She took the chance. She told me.

"In my dreams, you're him," she said. "And you're..." she struggled to think of the right word, "...dead."

"I'm him?" I asked. "What do you—" But the question died on my lips.

*I* was playing the part of the Corentin in her *dreams?*

"I don't understand. How can I be the Corentin?"

"I don't know," she said. "But in the dreams, you are." She tore her gaze away, stared at her feet. "No glow."

No glow. No life. No goodness in me at all.

I sat back into the dirt, sighing.

"What do you mean I'm 'dead'?" I finally asked.

At this question, her eyes fell, and he lower lip began to tremble. She didn't answer.

"Do you know it's not real?" I asked.

She looked up.

"But it is real," she argued, her voice quiet.

"No," I said. "It's just a dream."

But as I said the words, I remembered the black cloud that had covered her irises just hours ago. All of this was all too real. For her.

"He's trying to manipulate you," I said.

"What's manipu—?"

"He's trying to trick you," I explained. "He's trying to make you think I'm dead, or I'm him, or anything horrible that he wants you to think so that he can control you."

But my words were too much. I knew they were the truth, and I didn't have a good lie to tell her anyways. But the difference between the truth and what she needed to hear were two very different things.

*She's just a kid.*

Suddenly, guilt flooded through me. Here I was, forcing this little kid to accompany me on a journey that could very well mean the death of us both. That had never been my intention. I had meant to bring Cait here to protect her, to leave her with Mom back at the farm so that I could ensure her safety.

Now, I was dragging her along, and there was no protection for her out here except the tiny bit I could offer. Yes, the point was to fix it all, to balance the fold, to use her talents to lead me to the destination I so desperately needed to reach.

But I was using her.

Just like the Corentin.

Now I was the one fighting back tears.

"You don't have to come with me," I said. "I can take you back right now. I'll leave you with Mom and Grandma. Maybe you guys can stay with Lily for a while."

Her face brightened at the sound of her new friend's name, then fell again.

"No," she said. "I want to come with you."

"You do?" I choked. "Why?"

"Because you're the brightest one," she said.

"What do you mean?"

"Your glow is getting brighter." Her face was matter of fact. Honest.

"Brighter?" How was that possible? "Aren't you mad I took you along?" I asked.

She looked up at me, her eyes big and thoughtful.

"You're Rhainn's friend," she said. It was the first time I had heard her call him by his real name, not the sing-song nickname she usually used.

And something inside my chest seemed to break at her words. I couldn't decide if I wanted to cry or scream or deny her, tell her that she had been wrong.

I had failed Rhainn so badly.

"There's something I need to tell you," I said. "I told Rhainn I would go back for him. I told him I could save you both. But the Coyle got to him before I could. It's my fault he's gone." The words came out in a rush of tears as the weight of what I was facing, what I *had* faced, bore down on me.

"Did you lie?" she asked, looking at me sidelong, searching for the truth in my face.

201

"No, but—"

"I don't like it when people lie," she said.

I shook my head.

"I didn't lie."

"Then it's not your fault," she said. "He's still there." She looked up into the gray above.

I looked up, too. The sky lacked all color. Our world was now nothing but haze and sand.

Was Rhainn still alive, then? Could she feel him now?

I let my chin fall to my chest. I still had so much I needed to do, so much that seemed I was the only one able to do. But I had felt on the verge of falling apart for so long, I wondered if I would be able to even take another single step along the road I'd been traveling. A road that, with every bit of progress I made, made me feel more and more sure of the danger that awaited me on the other side.

My father, already possessed, was my destination.

Would I ever find him?

Suddenly, she was the one comforting me.

"Don't worry," she said, patting me on the cheek with her fat little hand. "We'll find your Daddy."

My breath caught in my chest, and I found I couldn't breathe at all anymore. In that moment, my mind had been filled with demons and gold and Jade's black eyes. But Cait's vision had pierced through it all, right to my heart.

"I can see him now," she said. "We're a lot closer than we were." She looked around again, trained her gaze westward.

Her magic knew. Her entire being knew. She knew it, understood it, accepted it.

She wrapped her arms around my neck and lay her head on my shoulder.

I hugged her, laughing and crying at the same time. Until that moment I had felt so lost.

Now I was found.

# CHAPTER TWENTY

We spent the next few days alternating between walking and jumping. Using the link became harder as we pressed on, not because it was losing power, but because of the toll it took on our bodies. Occasionally, I would become tense, suddenly eager again to make our destination as quickly as possible. I always felt that the Corentin was right behind us, that he would discover us at any moment and somehow wrench Cait, my only friend in this lonely place, from me. During these fits of worry, we would jump for hours, covering hundreds of miles as I tried to put distance between us and the mountains, the last place I had truly sensed his presence.

And the farther we got from the village, the better Cait seemed. Her nightmares hadn't returned, and I hadn't so much as seen a single wisp of black around the edges of her eyes since that first morning we had jumped away. I wondered if we had truly cast the Corentin off our trail.

Or if he knew precisely where we were and was just biding his time until the moment to strike was right.

This feeling of foreboding increased with each passing day, with each step we took. But gradually, the urge I felt to rush dissipated, turning to caution. A sort of calm started to settle over me, and I began to accept the fact that I couldn't control whatever it was that was the Corentin was planning next. Maybe it was the starkness of the terrain. Maybe it was the respite from attack. I felt, though, that the inevitable would happen, with or without my panic.

Cait grew quieter as the days passed, too, more focused. Whatever trail it was she was following seemed to take up all her attention, and instead of making the chatter I had become so familiar with, she now walked along in silence, her gaze locked on the horizon.

Finally, five days after our departure, a vast range of mountains rose up before us in the distance. Cait saw them first, probably right at the moment they had become visible through the haze. The silence from her lack of footsteps brought me out of my thoughts, and I turned to find her staring past me at the destination beyond. I walked back to stand beside her, kneeling down so that I could try to see the terrain from her level.

"That's where he is," she breathed. Her face was calm, but had an odd sadness about it I didn't understand.

"What's wrong?" I asked.

She looked at me, her face so full of pity that it sent a pang of foreboding through my center.

"I don't think he's..." she began, turning again to face the mountains.

She did not finish her thought.

"What?" I pressed. "What is it?"

"I think he's sick," she said.

Sick?

Was she seeing the same madness I, myself, had known so many years ago?

My fear was starting to bubble to the surface again, threatening the calm I had been building inside my mind. I shoved it back down, unwilling to face whatever truth would greet me when we finally found him.

If he was sick, then I'd just have to take care of him the best I knew how.

But the memory of Cait's black eyes still ate at me. The list of people needing help seemed to be growing, piling up in my wake as I went from place to place, pursuing the one goal I knew the Corentin wanted to keep me from attaining.

I changed the subject.

"How do you know where to go?" I asked, standing back up. It wasn't that I didn't trust her, it was that I was curious.

She glanced at me, clearly trying to wipe the pity off her face as she looked at me, then began walking again.

"I told you," she said. "I just see it."

"Okay," I said, giving her a playful nudge on the shoulder. "What does it look like then?"

Her face cracked into a smile, the first one I had seen from her in days. I returned it, noticing how oddly at ease it made me feel just to allow myself to smile. She stopped walking again, beckoning for me to kneel down to her once more. I did so, and together we stared out across the last of the flat plains between us and my father.

"It's like a trail," she said, pointing her finger out before her as if drawing a map in midair right along our path. "It changes sometimes, but usually it's sort of sparkly. Gold. Like dust."

I watched her hand as she outlined the path, over and over, a sort of swirling line that led from us to him.

"Yours is the brightest one I've seen."

"Why?" I asked.

She shrugged, letting her hand drop back down to her side.

"Most people just want things," she said. "But you really want to find him."

For some reason this brought to mind Brendan's diary. I hadn't looked through it since before Denver, but the stories he had recorded in those pages still followed me wherever I went.

Brendan had wanted to get home. He had felt obligated to complete his task, his duty, and return to his family.

But part of him, a part that grew as his years trapped on Earth dragged on, didn't want to leave at all. Hadn't he said again and again that he couldn't imagine life without Josephine and the children? I wondered if, in the end, his hesitation at leaving them behind had affected his ability to go at all. If his lack of wanting to go with his whole heart had somehow grounded him, rendering his attempt to use the magic insufficient.

I wondered if my desire to find my dad, which seemed to be growing with every second that ticked past, meant that I really would have an easier time finding him.

Suddenly, I couldn't wait to get there.

I held out one hand, and Cait looked up at me, taking it.

"I'm sick of walking," I said. "What do you say we just get this over with?"

She tore her eyes away from the mountains, met mine. Then, let out a big sigh.

"Okay," she said. "Let's do it."

Not for the first time, I was pushing her to do something she didn't really want to do. Though at least she didn't seem frightened like she had before. In fact, fear hadn't crossed her face at all since that first day on our own. Realizing this calmed me, and I turned to take in the mountains, myself. Somewhere up there, my father awaited. I wondered if he knew that I was coming for him. If he had any sense of what was happening in the world around him, or the worlds far off.

Or if, like Jade and so many before her, he was already lost within the grasp of the Corentin's evil.

By evening, we were high in the Sierras. That morning we had finished off the last of our water, carrying now just the empty plastic jug I had taken from Grandma's bag before we had left. I had counted on finding water in the mountains, but I hadn't thought it all the way through. Somehow, I had expected these mountains to resemble the Rockies we had just come from. Vast and wild and mostly uninhabited, but full of life and opportunity for food and water.

But these were not the Rockies.

What I had failed to realize, to connect in my brain, was the fact that it hadn't rained in the western part of the country for decades. Just because we were up high, safe from the haze, didn't mean we would easily find everything we needed. Now, as we stood on the jagged peak of one of the many mountains and looked out across the range, I realized that we were in more danger than that which the Corentin's pursuit brought.

The place looked like a bomb had been dropped here. The trees, millions of them, still stood, blanketing the mountains that stretched for miles in every direction. But the green needles I had expected to see draped from their branches were long gone, withered and fallen, probably long before I was born. My tongue moved across my dry, cracked lips as I searched helplessly for some sign of water. But everywhere I looked I saw nothing but rock, sand, and the long-forgotten skeletons of trees, a memory of what the world once was.

Cait was sitting in the dirt, too tired from the jumps to do anything but stare blankly into space. I knelt before her and gripped one of her ankles, pulling it gently to stretch out the taught muscles of her calves. She lay back in the dirt, groaning. I moved to her other leg, and after that each of her arms in turn. Finally, she sat up, pointing.

"It's not far," her voice croaked. Her lips were as dry as mine, and I watched as her tongue stuck out, trying to wet them.

"I think we should keep going," I said. The sun was setting already over the mountaintops, and a thought had occurred to me sometime in the past hour.

*If Dad's up here, he must have water.*

I only knew two things for sure. My father was somewhere in these mountains. And he was still alive. Cait wouldn't have been able to see the connection if he had been dead, I was certain of that. If he had been here for all the months we thought, he must have found a way to survive. He *had* to have water.

"How many more jumps, do you think?" I asked.

She stared into the distance, but I wondered if she saw anything at all. I was surprised when she answered.

"Two more," she said.

"Two jumps?" I asked.

"Yes."

She got back to her feet, seeming eager now, herself.

We jumped.

209

She adjusted the trajectory of the direction I pointed the link. We jumped again.

Nothing.

This entire forest, what felt like this entire world, was covered in the same, dead mass of branches and fallen needles, blown into dust by the relentless wind that whipped across the mountain range. My heart fell.

But Cait perked up. She set off away from me, walking down the mountain as if she had made this same journey a hundred times. Intrigued, I followed, my stomach picking up a flock of butterflies as I realized who was at the end of this hike.

Soon, we came to a clearing, and several buildings came into view. The place had been hidden by a rise in the side of the rock, but now each structure was revealed.

I wanted to stop, wanted to stand there for a while and let my mouth hang open with the disbelief I felt. Now that we were here, I allowed myself to realize the truth, that I hadn't been entirely sure Cait would be able to get us here at all. I had been desperate, thinking that maybe I could turn us back towards home if we failed. Part of me hadn't really believed, not for sure, that one five-year-old little girl would be able to find a place so remote, so specific, without adult help.

Now here we were.

But where *was* here?

In no time, she was at the base of the hill. Remnants of a gravel driveway crunched beneath her feet, and she turned back to see what was taking me so long, impatient.

"Come on!" she yelled.

I broke into a run, unable to contain my excitement any longer.

Together, we approached the largest building. Signs hung from the outer walls, indicating restrooms, entrance, a gift shop.

"Wait," I said, pointing to the sign hanging from the bathroom door. I pushed it open, and a pile of dust that had gathered from the crack beneath the door floated around the room. I turned the tap on the faucet, desperately hoping for anything, even just a trickle of water.

But nothing came out.

I checked the toilets, just to be sure, and when I found them dry I tried the other bathroom, the drinking fountains, every possible source of water I could find.

Finally, when it was clear that we were going to stay thirsty, I let my shoulders fall with disappointment and moved on. Cait, less perturbed by our lack of drinking water, skipped up ahead to the main entrance.

The front door, clearly having been forced open some time ago, stood ajar. I paused, watching Cait's little feet disappear around the corner. Then, with a feeling that was half terror, half excitement, I followed.

I ran after her, suddenly feeling like a very young child.

"Dad?" I called. My voice sounded younger than I would have liked.

No answer. I turned, walking through a long hallway. Cait had paused, staring around, and seeing we were alone, I did the same.

The whole place was covered floor to ceiling with framed photographs. Men. Hundreds of different men, the photos taken during different years. They sat in rows, some wearing helmets, some holding pickaxes. A few smiled. Most stared stoically ahead into the lens of the camera.

Something about those faces held me transfixed, and I couldn't move from the space as I looked deep into every face.

1932.

1918.

1938.

With a shudder, I realized that every single one of them was now dead.

And I realized what this place was.

It was a gold mine.

# CHAPTER TWENTY-ONE

I wasn't surprised. Not exactly.

But I was impressed with the size of the place. This was no small hole cut in the side of a mountain. This place was huge.

"Aster!" Cait shouted from some other passageway. I hadn't even realized she had left my side. My heart thudded as I followed the sound of her voice. Had she found him?

"Cait?" I called.

The space was dim, and I had to use my hands to feel along the wall towards her.

"I'm back here," she said, very close now.

My breathing caught in my chest. Somewhere back here Cait had found my father. I was sure of it. Any moment now we would be staring at each other for the first time in more years than I could remember. I tried to think of what to say, but my mind stayed blank as I inched along the corridor.

Slowly, something came into view. At first I gasped, thinking it was him, but as I got closer I found I couldn't put my finger on what it was I was seeing. A thin shaft of light was shining through the open doorway. I bumped into Cait in the darkness.

"Where—?" I began, but I was unable to finish the thought. Why hadn't he spoken?

"Look," she said.

My chest deflated as I realized it wasn't my father she had found, but something else entirely. But when I saw what it was, my heartbeat resumed with a vigor and, oddly, fear.

Before us stood a huge pane of glass, shattered from floor to ceiling. Aside from the point of impact, most of the pane stuck together like an enormous puzzle of glass shards. Behind it, several photographs stood propped against the back wall.

Photographs of gold.

Several large rocks, some the size of grapefruits, were once displayed here. The bases on which they had rested were empty, but the photographic proof remained.

"These are pictures," I said, my voice quiet. "Photographs. Remember when I told you about photographs?"

Beside me Cait sucked in her breath, understanding.

I stepped aside, to allow more light to reach the images. If only we had gotten here sooner. If only the huge stones that had once been here were now in our possession. We could leave this dead place and be done with it. It would have been more gold than I had ever seen in my entire life. More than, I felt sure, anyone in the Fold had ever seen. More than Almara or Brendan or Kiron or anyone ever could have dreamed of finding.

The rocks in the images were rough, unrefined and displayed in their original state. The biggest image, the one in the center, showed a stone that reminded me of a sea creature, its tiny tendrils stretching out from the center as if the gold was a creature searching for oxygen.

It was breathtaking.

This had once been a safe. These stones, so valuable both then and now, had been taken from it by force. It must have been a display case when this place had been a museum. A heavy metal door stood ajar, but the glass had once protected the contents of the giant vault. Now, a thousand tiny pieces of it lay strewn about the floor, and a hole just large enough for a greedy hand to reach through was punctured through the center of the pane. I wondered who had taken the gold. Why they had thought to. Between starvation and acid rain, wouldn't the thief only have had basic survival on their minds?

But the thing that caught my attention most, that had me itching to break through the rest of the glass, was not the old images of the gold that had once sat on these shelves.

It was the large framed map that rested behind where they had once sat.

*Copper Creek Gold Mine,* the little placard glued to the front of the glass read. An intricate lattice of lines ran up and down the map, showing where the most valuable tunnels had been dug into the mountain. We might have missed the opportunity to snatch the larger stones that had once rested here, but with a map like that we would be well on our way to finding the rest of the gold we needed.

I folded my hand into a fist and tapped it on the glass remaining in the door frame. Surprisingly, it rattled in its frame. It was clearly heavy, but not well set. I was surprised that the treasure that had once been encased here had been protected by nothing but a thick pane of glass.

I wanted that map.

But I didn't want to shred my arm against the jagged glass the thief had left behind.

I thought of the men in the photographs, some of them holding pickaxes.

"Wait a minute," I said, thinking. "If this place is a mine, there must be tools around here someplace. Come on."

I turned and ran from the room. As I rounded the corner into the entryway, I squinted as the brightness of day stung my eyes.

"Where are you going?" Cait asked.

"We need some tools," I explained.

I ran through the gift shop, still stocked with tiny samples of gold that must have come from this very mine. I paused, then dashed behind the counter, collecting the little trinkets and stuffing them into my pocket. It wasn't much, barely enough to make a link or two, but every little bit would help. Then, when I had every minuscule gold nugget I could find, I headed for the door.

Outside we found more buildings scattered around the place. Workshops of all sorts dotted the landscape, and my heart thudded as I recognized a variety of metal tools, once displayed as artifacts, still intact. No rain had fallen here in ages, and the tools were in relatively good condition.

I grabbed for the first one I saw, a large pickaxe with a pointed end, and headed back inside. Cait, who seemed to be thinking marginally more clearly than I was, grabbed a couple of helmets with battery powered lights set into the brims and followed behind. She had seen the pictures of the men, I realized, some of whom had their helmet lanterns lit.

When we walked back through the gift shop, she twisted a little dial on the helmets. One of them came to life, a dim, wide beam of light shining from the attached headlamp. She held it out to me, then shook the other helmet, tapping on the side of the bulb. I laughed.

"I guess you're getting used to electronics, after all," I teased.

She glanced up, smirking, but could not get the helmet to light.

"It's okay," I said. "We'll just use this one for now."

I put the helmet on my head, feeling like an idiot, but being too focused to care much. With the ax in one hand and Cait's hand in my other, I walked back through to the gold room.

I paused for a moment. Something about this place was so silent, so precious. It was almost like being in a church, long abandoned.

But I couldn't wait forever.

"Get back," I said, and Cait took several steps backwards.

I raised the axe over my head, got ready to swing.

"Wait!" Cait cried.

I paused, irritated.

"What?" I growled. I had been so close.

"What if the glass shatters?" she asked. "Your eyes."

I hadn't thought of that, and immediately I regretted my impatience. I looked around the room, lit now by the faint glow of the headlamp. There was nothing here I could use to shield my eyes from shards of glass, though. Then, a thought popped into my head, and I snorted with laughter.

"What?" she asked.

"Come on," I said, gesturing for her to follow me.

I led her back to the doorway.

"Turn around, and cover your eyes, okay?" I said. "If it blows out, the glass could make it this far."

She did as I instructed, holding one hand up over each eye as she scooted herself farther out into the adjacent room.

I raised the ax again, but this time my posture was different, calculated. It was a stance I had learned many months ago, back in a forest clearing, with an old friend I'm sure never dreamed I could use the skills he was teaching me for something as wild as this.

I pictured a tree, wide and fat, before me. The ax felt too weighted on one end, and I adjusted it automatically. I imagined the cracks in the tree bark where in reality there was only glass. And I let the ax fly.

The ax rocketed across the room with great speed, and when it hit the glass, the pane did not shatter.

*Chink.*

The heavier side of the blade stuck into the glass, just as it might if it really had been thrown at a tree trunk.

I laughed, happy that my old talent for ax throwing was still with me.

"You can open your eyes," I said, walking back into the room.

I grabbed the ax handle and began wrenching it out of the glass. It had stuck fast into the shattered glass, but the pieces hadn't broken free. Some sort of film had been applied, either to keep the shards from hurting people in the event that the glass was broken, or to deter thieves, making them think the glass would be more trouble than it was worth.

It didn't deter me.

I wrestled with the handle, pulling and pushing on the glass until, finally, a piece of it two feet square peeled away out of the frame in one big sheet of diamond shards.

"We're going to do this," I said, my stomach fluttering with excitement.

Cait was just opening her mouth to speak, when an ear splitting sound echoed throughout the room. It rattled within my skull, so loud I felt sure it would turn my brain to mush. An alarm. I dropped the ax and held my hands over my ears. Cait did the same. I stared around, looking for the source of the offending noise, but saw nothing.

"Come on!" I shouted over the blaring, and I made for the exit.

Once outside, I let my hands drop away, sticking my fingers in my ears and jiggling them around, as if by doing so I could stop the ringing I now heard.

"What was that?" she asked.

"An alarm," I said. I thought that maybe I was talking too loudly, but I could barely hear my own voice.

"What set it off?"

"We did," I said.

I looked around, trying to think of something to stuff into my ears so that I could go back in to retrieve the map. Then I saw the look on Cait's face, and I stopped my searching.

"What is it?" I asked.

Her eyes had gone wide and blank, and I felt sure she was seeing something only she could. She opened her mouth to speak, but no words came out.

"Is it—is it him?" I asked.

Slowly, she nodded. She turned, making her way not back into the building, but around it.

I followed, all of my intentions fading away like smoke from a fire. The safe. The gold. The alarm. The map.

For this task, no map was needed.

# CHAPTER TWENTY-TWO

I ripped the helmet from my head and thrust it over her straggly hair.

"You go first," I said. "I'm right beside you."

She walked, automatic and purposeful, her tiny feet crunching in the gravel below. Her gaze moved downward to the ground, and it struck me that, to her eyes, she was following an actual trail. The path that extended between me and my father was visible to her. Her pace quickened, and as she moved around the building, running one small hand along the rough stone edge of the structure. Then, as we turned the next corner, she broke into a run.

I followed, surprised by her sudden flight. As we ran, I scanned every dark corner, every hiding spot where he might be. But she went straight past each one, and moments later she wrenched open a door on the building opposite the shop and led me into a dark, musty space. As the metal door slammed behind us, we were thrust into near total darkness. Only the dim light of her headlamp and one tiny window illuminated the room, and we could barely see five feet in front of us.

The building was made of stone, built hundreds of years ago, I guessed. Everything smelled oddly of metal, and a large assortment of tools littered the floor.

This whole place must have been a museum before the drought. It hadn't just been in the first building, but had extended to the other structures that were scattered about. All around us, displays, long coated in a film of dust and cobwebs, sat where they had been placed for public viewing decades ago.

Cait continued, walking now down a wide staircase.

"Where are you taking me?" I asked.

She held up one shaking finger, pointed it towards the floor. Taking a few steps forward, her fingers found an iron gate, interlacing between the thin metal bars that kept us safe.

And what I saw took my breath away.

A track jutted forward from beneath our feet, and I let my eyes follow it as it descended down a steep hill, deep into the earth and out of sight. Somewhere in this cave, water dripped, and my tongue moved over my dry lips, suddenly reminding me of my thirst.

I stared down the hill again, rolling down, down, down.

It was the entrance to the mine.

"He's down there?" I asked.

I could barely see. My hands moved across the iron bars, and I was suddenly scared of falling down into the black abyss below. I found a handle and turned it. Then, realizing what it was, I opened the door and peered down at what lay beyond.

A long, seemingly endless staircase descended into the darkness, an emergency route built beside the track.

"I found it," I said. "This is how we get down."

I looked around and grabbed another helmet, prominently displayed to one side of the shaft. The light on it came to life instantly at my touch, and I breathed a sigh of relief as I jammed it onto my head.

"Down there?" I asked one last time. "You sure?"

Her gaze was still distant, but she heard my questions and nodded. I reached out for her hand, which she held out idly. Her body moved automatically, followed me without comment or complaint.

The walls of the shaft were at once refreshing and oppressive. The deeper we descended into the mine, the more cool and moist they became, and soon tiny drips of water ran down the cave walls on every side. I ran my hand along the moisture, licked at it desperately. Suddenly, my original purpose was forgotten, overrun by the primal need to find water.

I don't remember letting go of Cait's hand, but soon I was running down the steps, one hand sliding along the wall until I got far enough down to find a thin trickle. It only released a few drops at a time, but I stood there with my tongue pressed up against the wall like a dog. Two. Three. Four drops of water wet my mouth, and I licked my lips, tasting the mineral-rich condensation, a taste oddly like blood.

I became aware of movement behind me and turned to find Cait. For just those few moments I had forgotten her entirely. But she came down the steps at a steady rhythm, plodding down one foot after the next, her gaze focused on the blackness ahead.

I turned, watching her pass, that feeling of foreboding returning. Her movements were stilted, automatic.

*Automatic.*

I tried to breathe, but found my throat closed as if the Corentin himself had my neck in a vice grip. That blank stare. Her voice, now quieted.

A flood of panic and loss seemed to flow into my lungs like the water in the sea had that day I saved him.

I ran after her.

"Wait!" I shouted, flying so fast down the stairs I could barely stay upright. The light on my helmet caught the edge of her hand, and I shouted again. "Stop!"

She didn't stop. She just kept walking.

I rounded in front of her, put my hands on her shoulders, shook and shook her.

Every molecule of air came flooding out of me when I saw that her eyes were still clear. Still their pretty blue. Not a hint of wispy blackness around the edges.

*Just calm down.*

It took me a while to catch my breath. I felt jumpy, and now the sounds of water dripping suddenly seemed menacing as they echoed off the cavern walls. The sound of my own breathing made me nervous.

But Cait stayed still, only barely swaying on the spot where I held her back. Despite whatever turmoil was swirling silently within her, she remained calm, placid. She was no threat.

I looked back up the staircase, part of me longing to turn back now. Paranoia gripped me as I thought wildly that she could be leading me into a trap.

But then I thought about the girl I knew, and I realized that couldn't be. Something I wanted was at the end of this staircase, I was sure of it. Waiting for me at the bottom of this mine shaft. Gold. My father. Maybe death. But I had to press on. Nothing but misery waited for me in the world above if I quit now.

Cait simply stood, stared blankly ahead. Finally, knowing I had little other choice, I released her. She walked ahead, resuming her plodding pace as she stepped down the endless staircase.

It seemed like we walked for a long time. The muscles above my knees began to ache as we went, and soon I was wishing we were headed in the other direction just to bring relief. I looked over at the long track laid out in the gravel beside the staircase, and I idly wondered how we were going to get back out again. If we *would* get back out again.

Her ratty hair stuck out oddly from beneath the helmet as she continued down the stairs. With a pang I remembered the braid Carl had twisted into it just a few days ago, giving her the neat appearance of a well-tended child. Now that pretense was gone, and the truth walked ahead before me. Cait was an orphan, a slave to her own magic, the weird talent she had absorbed from the Hills of Elyso. I quietly sang her tune as we walked.

*"The child of Elyso looks at me*
*The child of Elyso sees my dreams*
*Through wind and rain and swirling hail*
*The child of Elyso finds the trail"*

I followed on. Soon, larger trickles of water snaked their way down the cavern walls. I stopped, an idea occurring to me. I dropped my pack and dug out our empty water jug. Then, just as Cait was fading into the blackness up ahead, I ran after her. Soon, I found another trickle along the wall. I held the container to it, all the time my eyes on Cait as she descended in her lost, stilted gait.

When she was nearly gone again, I flew down the stairs after her. I looked in the bottle. It seemed like I had maybe half a cup of liquid. I tilted back the jug and took the first whole mouthful of water I had had since yesterday. Then, I walked in front of her again, forcing her to stop. I gently took a fistful of her hair and tilted her head backwards. Her mouth opened slightly, and I trickled the remaining water into it. She sputtered and coughed, but she swallowed. Then, when every last drop of the container was down her throat, I let her go again. She moved on ahead as if nothing at all had happened.

We continued downward. Soon, a flickering light caught my attention up ahead. Fire? It couldn't be. There was no smoke in the tunnel. What was it then?

My lamp bobbed on my head as I trotted down a few steps in front of Cait, and the light I saw in the distance moved with it. I realized I was staring at a reflection, and a few moments later I saw why.

Water.

My feet splashed into it at the line where it met the steps, and I saw the whole cave was flooded. My heart leapt and fell at the same moment. Urgently, I dunked my water bottle into the cold, clear liquid and thrust it to my mouth, gulping it down. I ignored the nagging sensation in my gut, the part of me that questioned everything I came across.

Was this the end of our underground journey?

Where *was* he?

I turned, expecting to see Cait standing beside me, perhaps waiting for her next drink.

But she was gone.

"Cait?" I called, panic filling me.

I bounded up the steps, nearly missing the passageway that jutted off to one side. I turned just in time and saw the fading light of her headlamp as she continued walking, content to move on without my presence. I ran after her.

This cave was narrower, just barely high enough for me to move through it without hitting my head on the ceiling. Still, I crouched, not wanting to risk damaging the only light I had on the top of my helmet. If I were to get lost down here in the dark, I felt certain that even the straight shot back up the stairs would be enough to drive me insane with terror.

When I reached Cait, she was the same as she had been, driven to turn the corner by a force I couldn't hear or feel. I stopped her, my breath heaving with exhaustion and relief.

"Don't run off like that," I scolded, unsure if she could hear me through her haze.

I tilted her head back again. This time her lips automatically latched onto the jug, and she drank deeply. But it didn't do a thing for her consciousness. When she had drank her fill, she moved on again, like a ghost wandering endlessly through a tomb she could find no peace within. But soon more than just the faint sounds of our footsteps echoed off the narrow tunnel walls. In the distance, a faint tapping sounded.

For a moment I stopped, watched her move away from me towards the sound. Then, unexpectedly, my heart leapt, and I ran on in front of her. Water was flowing everywhere now; there must have been some sort of underground spring feeding the flooded tunnels. We were just above the level of the water, which trickled down the slightly declining path next to my feet. My boots splashed in the puddles that formed in the crevices of the rock, and the sound of clean water made me feel elated, hopeful. Any moment now. Maybe around the next turn. For the first time on this journey, the fear I felt, the worry about finding my father, disappeared.

And then he was there.

He stood with is back to me, wearing one of the helmets from the world above, just like we did, and tapping against the stone walls with a small chisel.

*Tink. Tink. Tink.*

I stopped, frozen.

His clothes were worn to rags, and they hung, dirty and torn, from his thin frame. Beneath his helmet, unkempt, blond hair stuck out at all angles. I could just barely make out the sheen of sweat on the side of his cheek as he worked.

This was it.

"Dad?" I asked. My voice was quieter than I would have liked.

He paused, turning slightly. Then, upon seeing the light from my helmet, spun all the way.

His light was brighter than mine, and it stung my eyes. I put one arm up, trying to shield myself.

"Who's there?" he asked. His voice was alarmed and oddly high pitched.

"It's me," I said. "It's Aster."

"Aster?" he asked. Suddenly his posture took on a new appearance. He braced himself against the rock wall, his hands fumbling over the stone behind him.

As if he were searching for a way out.

"Yeah," I said. "Don't you—don't you recognize me?"

In his fumbling, the chisel he had held in his right hand clattered to the floor of the cave. His breathing came hard and fast.

"You get away from me," he snarled, his voice cracking with fear as he tried to make it sound frightening.

I took another tentative step towards him, my heart sinking in my chest.

"What do you mean? I just wanted to—"

"You're *his*," he breathed. "You're all his, and I want no part of it. You can't have the gold, do you hear me? It's mine. I've spent years." He reached out with one foot and shuffled his pack so that it was situated behind him. The movement seemed to cost him great effort, and suddenly I wondered if it had been him to break through the glass above and steal the treasures of this once rich place.

"I'm not here to take anything from you," I said, pausing. Was that really true? "You're—you're sick. I can help you. I can help you fight him. The Corentin." I angled the light on my helmet, trying to see the color of his eyes. But the glare from his own lamp was too much; I could barely make out the features of his face while staring into that light.

"Sick?" he spat. "That's what they all say. But they're wrong. You load me up with your pills and your talk until I'm a zombie. That's your idea of *helping*."

A small hand gripped onto my arm, and I looked down to see Cait holding on tight, her vision cleared. She had brought me to my destination, and she was fully conscious again. And terrified.

"Dad, we're just kids," I said, gesturing to Cait. "We're not here to give you medicine. I can take you to the Fold. I've been there. I'm healed now, too. And if you'll just—"

"What did you say?" he asked, but not a hint of wonder echoed through his voice. He took a step towards me, and from the light of my headlamp I could see that his eyes, which I had expected to be dark with the black of the Corentin, were just as clear as Cait's.

He wasn't possessed.

I frowned, unsure.

If he wasn't possessed, then why was he looking at me that way? Like he wanted nothing more than to knock me to the ground?

"I said, I've been to the Fold, Dad. I found Almara. I met Brendan's sister. I can fix this."

But now I was the one backing away.

His eyes narrowed.

"I knew it," he said.

Something that looked like recognition flashed across his face, and he approached me, his arms outstretched. I felt trapped, unsure of his intention. Unsure of his state of mind. But I stood frozen at his approach, the little kid in me waiting to be swept up into his arms and hugged.

"I knew you'd come for me," he said.

Cait's hands squeezed against my arm.

And then, when those clear blue eyes were so close that I could see the flecks of gray in his irises, he reached out for me, a smile creeping up onto his face. He stretched out his arms as if to hug me. I paused, part of me wanting to flee, and another, deeper part of me desperately wanting to walk into his waiting embrace. Inside his arms, I might be able to forgive him, maybe even to forget.

I stepped closer, yearning for a connection with the man who had deserted me so long ago.

And he wrapped his hands, not around my shoulders.

But around my neck.

# CHAPTER TWENTY-THREE

His helmet toppled off his head, clanging to the floor, the sound making him jump. But before I could squirm out from beneath him, I felt his bony fingers lock against my windpipe again. I opened my mouth, intending to scream, but no sound came except for an involuntary gasping sound as my body fought against his hold. I gripped at his wrists, but no matter how hard I dug my fingernails into his skin, he wouldn't let go.

Cait jumped onto his back, biting and hitting with everything she had to try to get him off me. But he was a man possessed, maybe not yet by the Corentin, but by some other desire to kill off his only son. Fear? Greed? Every possibility whirled through my mind as he pushed me down onto the floor and squeezed.

I wished for my staff, regretted in that moment that I had traveled so far and left it behind, even if it might not have worked on such a faraway planet. I tried to call up my power without it, tried to see hope in the face that stared down at me now, sweat pouring from his forehead, dirt mashed into his beard, wildness deep within his sunken eyes.

There was hope. There had to be hope. There was always hope.

I told myself these things, and I believed them. But no magic came to me.

The room began to swim, and the tiny popping lights I had once seen when on the verge of death flashed in front of me.

Was this how it was going to end?

Cait was crying now, still fighting furiously against the rigid body of my father, gasps of frustration and panic coming from her throat as her little hands beat him in the best way she knew how.

"Aster!" she screamed. "No! No!"

She took fistfuls of his hair, tried desperately to stop him.

My father didn't even notice her attempts to thwart him, didn't even give her as much consideration as one might have given a fly buzzing around his head on a hot summer day.

*Pop, pop,* went the lights in front of my vision.

I looked deep into the eyes of my murderer. My creator. I willed him to see me, his son, and to come to his senses.

But the only reward I got made the blood in my veins turn to ice. I saw, instead, the inevitable.

Black wisps of smoke flitted into the corners of his eyes. I might have gasped if I had been able to. I might have looked away at this final moment if I had been able to turn my head.

But I could not gasp or look away. Instead, I watched as the smoke swirled around and around, gradually working its way into his irises until nothing but coal black stared back at me.

There was no one here to save me. No Kiron with his stew. No Jade with her elixir. It was over. The Corentin had finally, once again, caught up with me.

I closed my eyes then, waiting for death to finally come, wishing that

I had had the strength to somehow complete what I now saw was a near impossible task.

But instead of being launched into a cosmos full of stars as I had been in that cave with Cadoc so long ago, I felt a sensation I didn't expect.

Loosening.

I was dizzy. Even in the dark behind my eyelids, the world was a swirl of misery as my brain slowly lost oxygen. And then from out of nowhere, my throat opened up, automatically gasping for the breath of life that hovered just outside my mouth, just on the other side of his fingers blocking its flow.

But his fingers were gone now.

Every tiny pinprick of white swirled out of my vision like water running down a drain. I rolled over, gagging and coughing, heaving, my body fighting to survive. Between each gasp of air, I tried to make sense of what had just happened.

Had Cait fought him off somehow? Was her power greater than I had imagined?

But no. I looked up to see her concerned, frightened face staring down at me.

And him. He was across the tunnel, sitting with his back pinned up against the wall as if he had tried to get away, but had given up at the moment his back had met the stone.

Slowly, as my body shuddered and wheezed, I sat up. I looked towards the entrance to the small cave, imagined a world in which I might run away from whatever was about to happen next, but not only could I still barely breathe, I was weak from the attack. I sat waiting, staring at the man, wondering when he would come for me again.

But he didn't.

Finally, I spoke.

"Go on, then," I said. The sound of my voice was a croak, and speaking hurt from the damage to my windpipe. My words were those of a man confronting death himself.

"I'm sorry, what?" he said. His eyes, still burning black, looked back at me quizzically, almost as if he had only just noticed me there.

"Kill me," I said. "Get it over with. I'm done." I slumped back down to the ground.

"Aster, no!" Cait wailed. She flung her arms around me, tried to force me to hug her, to comfort her as I had in recent days.

So many times on this journey I had expected to find him. Sometimes I had wanted nothing more than to look into the face of the man who had abandoned me. Sometimes I wanted to run full speed in the other direction. Now, finally here sitting across from him, I just wanted it to be over.

He was not the man I expected. He was not the man I wanted.

He looked down at his hands, as if only a vague memory of what he had been in the middle of doing still existed within his foggy brain.

"I'm not going to kill you," he said. His voice was clear and kind, not the voice I had come to associate with the Corentin.

"Yes you are," I said, closing my eyes. I patted Cait's head as her tears fell drop by drop onto my cheeks. "It's okay, Dad. Just do it."

"Dad?" he asked. "I don't know what you're talking about."

I peeked out from behind one of my eyelids. It had to be another Corentin trick, I thought.

He moved towards me on all fours.

"Are you alright?" he asked. "What happened to you?"

*What?*

"You tried to kill me," I spat. "That's what happened to me." I opened my eyes fully now.

He frowned, one hand outstretched in midair, a gesture of help.

"Are you kidding me?" I asked. I sat up and Cait promptly sat down in my lap, nestling into the one place she could find protection from the world around her.

But something very strange was happening, and I feared neither of us would find protection within these walls.

Then, Cait perked up, staring at him as if it were the first time she had seen him.

"Where did he go?" she asked, staring back and forth between him and me. Her eyes were wide and more amazed than fearful.

"He's right there," I said.

*Waiting to kill me. Tormenting me. Just like always.*

"No, he's not," she argued. She tilted her head, examining him from across the cave. "He's changed."

She wiped away the tears on her face, which had suddenly ceased coming.

"He's possessed," I spat. "It's only a matter of—"

Then, Cait slipped out from beneath my arms and approached him, still looking at him in that strange way.

"It's you," she said. "You were the one I followed here."

My heart sank. If Cait believed that the Corentin was our friend...

My mind and heart wrestled with the fact, though, that Cait had never steered me wrong. Not intentionally.

Not unless she, herself was possessed.

But her eyes were clear as she stared between us, and I knew that whatever she must be seeing was real.

"It was *his* trail I followed," she said. "He's the one you wanted to find."

"What are you talking about?" I asked, incredulous. "I did not want to find my father possessed by the most evil being in the cosmos!"

Now it was me she tilted her head at, concerned.

"But he's not," she said. "I can see him."

"What?"

"The glow," she said, reaching out one hand and taking his. Then, looking at him very seriously, she said, "I don't like the other one."

The other one?

"What is she talking about?" I asked him.

"I don't know," he said.

"What's your name?" I asked.

"I'm—well, I don't know," he said.

"How long have you been down here?"

He shrugged, shaking his head.

"I think maybe I just got here today," he said. "I—I'm sorry. I don't really remember."

Then, he crawled away, back towards his pile of belongings.

"Can I get you something for that?" he asked, pointing to my neck.

*He doesn't remember?*

He rummaged through an old, black backpack, the type hikers wore, searching for what I didn't know. I peered over at him, unable to help myself and my curiosity, and my vision caught a flash of something as he jostled his pack about.

Gold.

I gasped again, trying too late to stifle the sound.

He turned, perplexed. Then, seeing my eyes fixed on the enormous stone, he picked it up and brought it over to me.

"It's gold," he said, kneeling down in front of me. He heaved it over towards me, where it landed with a *thunk* on the cave floor.

I backed away at first, anticipating another attack. But no attack came, and my curiosity got the better of me. The stone was huge, and clearly heavy. He placed it on the floor before me as if it were worth little more than an ordinary rock, and I saw with near certainty that it was the largest of the stones in the museum pictures somewhere above our heads.

"I've been searching for gold," he said. He looked at the stone, a confused expression on his face. "I'm pretty good at it, too," he said.

"Why?" I asked.

He shrugged again. "I don't know," he said. "I hear a voice sometimes." He lifted one hand to his temple, swirled a single finger around and around on the skin. "It leads me from place to place."

"And you don't even know why?" I asked.

I didn't know what was going on, but somehow the possession wasn't taking hold of him. Somehow, in the middle of my own murder, he had forgotten what he was supposed to do.

What was going on?

"Dad, that's the Corentin's voice. You have to get away from him. You have to fight him."

But in that moment, remembering that the man with the clear eyes had been the one to attack me, and this one who was clearly possessed was as docile as a house pet, I backed away again.

"Why do you call me 'Dad'?" he asked. "I don't have any children."

The whole world seemed to be collapsing around me. Nothing made any sense. The dizziness was fading away now, but the confusion remained.

I scrambled away, seeking an exit.

His face fell, clearly frustrated.

"Here," he said. "You take it. I can always find more. Will that help you?" He reached over and pushed the great gold stone in my direction.

I paused.

"Are you serious?" I asked. No Corentin I had ever known would part with a gift of such immense value.

"You seem to want it," he said. "I mean, why else would you be down in a gold mine." He chuckled at the joke, but he was the only one. Then, staring around the room for a moment, and then back at me, he asked, "Did I really do that to you?"

It was too much. My own father had just tried to kill me. Then, possessed, he had stopped, suddenly no longer able to remember who I was or even his own name. And now he was acting as if we were casual acquaintances at a dinner party or something.

Suddenly, every emotion I was feeling seemed to bubble to the surface all at one time.

"Yes, you did this to me!" I screamed, my voice still hoarse. "This is all your fault! Everything! The Fold! My heart! The Corentin! It's all your fault!"

I knew it wasn't true. How could it be? But the words felt good coming out as hot tears splashed down my face.

"You left us!" I bellowed on, getting to my feet. "All alone on this stinking, dying planet! And for what? Because you wouldn't take your medicine? You're a horrible man. I know he's in there. I know he has you right now. And he's waiting. Just sitting there waiting for me to let my guard down so you can attack me again. Well, go ahead then!" I took a few steps towards him, and he backed away along the ground. "It's what you want, isn't it? For me to be dead? It's what you've both wanted all along!"

It felt so good to blame him for everything, for every tiny prick of pain that I had been forced to endure since he had left us. I stood there, spent and heaving, waiting for him to come at me again.

But he didn't.

"I don't want anybody dead," he said quietly after a time. "I don't even know who you are. I mean, you look a bit familiar. Something about the hair." His fingers twiddled with his own blond, dirty mop of hair. "But you're not my *son*. Are you? Is that possible?"

I was reeling again, trying to figure out what was real and what was imaginary, what was true and what was trick. I melted back down to the floor. Somewhere behind me, Cait grabbed hold of my arm, clinging to me, her only friend in this strange and terrifying world.

"Cait," I said, trying hard to keep my voice calm. "What do you see?" She looked up at me, still concerned, but no longer frightened. "When you look at him. What do you see?"

She peeked out from behind my embrace, staring at the confused man who sat across from us now. My murderer? My father? My enemy? Which choice would she make?

Which choice would I?

She untangled herself from my arms and moved towards him, staring hard all the while. She took a couple of steps in his direction, then extended one hand to him.

My breath caught in my chest as I waited, certain that he would show his true colors in this instant, that the truth would be revealed in his actions.

But he just sat there, staring mildly up at her, the girl who had led me to him at last. Then, after several long moments, their eyes locked onto each other, he raised his hand and slipped it into hers.

And when she turned back to me, her eyes couldn't have been clearer, couldn't have been purer.

"I see gold."

# CHAPTER TWENTY-FOUR

I backed away. It was all too much. So I did what I always did.

I ran.

I didn't know what was real anymore or who to believe. Cait, herself, had been possessed by the Corentin just days ago. Did that mean that her opinion of my father held any less weight? Could it be that the words from her mouth were nothing more than a trick, a sprouted seed planted by the Corentin long before now?

All I knew was that, in that moment, I didn't care. I couldn't face the truth, whatever it was, because everything was so muddled. I had counted on things being black and white. Easy. He was either crazy or he wasn't. He was either possessed by the evil madman or he wasn't. He either loved me or he didn't.

But in this new reality it seemed like all of those things were true in some way.

And I couldn't take it.

I flew up the stairs, pushing and pushing my screaming legs to climb faster. Far in the distance, the fading evening light cast a twilight glow through the tiny window at the top. I had to get there. I had to get out of here.

*You don't have the gold.*

I didn't care. I was through with this. I was no champion. I may have had some powers in the Fold, but they were useless here on Earth. I was helpless to fight for my family. For Cait. For my own life, even.

I imagined breaking through the entrance at the top of the shaft, jumping to the tallest peak I could find. Maybe I would leap from it once I got there. Maybe I would leave this all behind for other people to handle. If I was gone, the Corentin would have to find new people to torment. New victims to play out his sick games with.

But not me.

I couldn't do it anymore.

Soon, I was gasping for breath, my chest burning as if it were on fire. For the first time since I had made that very first jump to the Triaden, I felt my lungs protesting, seizing. I stopped the climb, both hands over my heart, suddenly certain that this would be the death of me.

Fine, then. One less thing I would have to worry about accomplishing. I was a failure. I deserved a failure's death.

Exhausted, I fell backwards to the rough stone steps. Automatically, I held up the water jug to my lips, drinking deeply.

I let the jug fall to my feet and put my head in my hands. Tears, this time of total hopelessness, washed the dirt from my face.

I didn't want to die.

But I couldn't see how I could go on living. Not like this.

They had all fallen. One by one, the people that I loved had fallen. More would follow. Nobody would be spared. Not in the end. In the end, the planets would collide, and every last one of them would die.

With a pang of guilt I remembered Cait, still somewhere at the bottom of this old mine, left with no one to protect her against the madman who didn't know his own name. But in that moment I felt helpless to think of anyone but myself, and she had made a choice I couldn't agree with. I could understand how she could have looked into Corentin black and seen good. I couldn't believe her. I was powerless to help Rhainn or to protect Cait against all of this, no matter what promises I had made.

I could stay on Earth. I could hide. At the end of the world where no rain fell, I could sit and wait for my end to come. No effort required.

I felt drained, and I understood now why hope had been the power that fueled my magic. Without it, I was nothing. I was empty. A deflated balloon.

Time passed, though I couldn't tell how much. Had hours gone by? Minutes? I turned off my headlamp and sat in the total darkness of the shaft, waiting for answers to come to me, for the truth to come to the surface of my brain. Alone in the dark, I tried to recall the feeling of hope that had lent its strength to my magic. But now, not only did I feel lost, I felt helpless to solve the puzzle of what was happening within these very walls. It was a riddle I couldn't understand, and I just wanted it all to end. Slowly, I let myself fade into darkness, only barely feeling the edge of my helmet crunch against the rock stair as I lay on the stairs, exhausted and spent.

I didn't hear them coming, but the lights flitted around the corners of my mind as they took step after arduous step towards the surface. Towards me. Soon, big hands were lifting me up by the shoulders, putting me on my feet. When my legs didn't obey, he slung one of my arms over his shoulders and helped to hoist me up the stairs.

I felt dizzy, too overwhelmed to bother forcing myself up on my own steam, too exhausted to speak, to do anything but allow myself to be dragged along. He was carrying nearly my entire weight, but he pressed on without complaint. Dimly, I wondered if the Corentin's possession gave him additional strength. Yes, that would be it. Cait had nearly killed me when the black had clouded her eyes, and she was tiny. A man of his size under the same spell could certainly handle a few stairs with me in tow.

He spoke, but I couldn't understand what he said. I only heard his voice, sounding like a mumble as it slowly penetrated the fog I was stuck within.

"...going home..." it said, "...together now..."

I wanted to fight, to argue, to fling his hands off me, now so oddly helpful. Then, as we neared the top, I heard it.

"It'll be okay, Aster."

It was Cait. Her hand patted the side of my face, an echo of my mother's touch on her own.

Slowly, my mind began to focus, and as we pushed through the outer door at the top of the shaft, I was finally able to speak.

"What now?" I asked.

She looked up at me, her eyes calm and blue and full of a lifetime of knowledge, more than any child her age should have bourn.

"We go home," she said. "We find Rhainn."

She glanced towards my father as if looking for reassurance. They must have spoken after I had left, devised a plan. He moved me over towards a low wall, and I slumped down onto it. Part of me wanted to thank him, to talk to him, to find out more about what had happened, what was *happening*, to him. But another part, a much bigger part, was terrified to even look at him. I felt certain that if I looked into those clouded eyes again, I would find nothing but the Corentin staring back at me.

Soon, I found I didn't have a choice.

He flipped my headlamp on, and took off his own helmet. Then he sat down across from me.

My skin crawled at his closeness.

"Look at me," he said.

I stared down at my hands, too scared to move.

"Aster, is it?" he pressed. "Look at me."

Slowly, I let my eyes lift, found his.

But nothing had changed. They stormed, dark and cloudy, just as they had down beneath the rock. Just as Cait's had the day she tried to kill me. Just as Jade's.

I dropped my gaze again.

"What do *you* want to do?" he asked.

The world was spinning again, and the little strength I had regained from hearing Cait's voice drained away.

"We should leave," he said. "Maybe if we get away from here, you'll feel better."

Something I'd forgotten suddenly swam up to the surface.

"Where's the gold?" I mumbled, blinking heavily.

"I have the gold," he said. From the side of his backpack, he retrieved that stone I had seen in the safe, the salvation of all of us. He lifted up the huge rock.

I tried to force myself to focus on him, but I couldn't do it.

I reached out for the gold, and was surprised when he let it drop into my hands easily. He didn't seem to mind handing over the treasure he had stolen for his master one bit. The stone was heavy, and I stared down at the tiny threads that stuck out of it on every side, ever reaching.

"How are you so…normal?" I asked.

He snorted with laughter, a sound so unexpected that it jarred me, making me marginally more alert.

"I want to know," I said, trying and failing to give my voice the sort of command that would inspire his honesty.

"I don't really know," he said, looking up at the twilight sky. He paused for several long moments, seemingly trying to figure out how to phrase his thoughts. "Do you ever get the feeling that you're walking around in a haze?" he finally asked. "Like everything you do is automatic? Like you're on autopilot?"

I nodded.

"Well, I've been like that for a long time, I think," he continued. I feel sort of…new. Like a newborn child. I vaguely remember coming here months ago. Though I seem to be sharing this body with another; I don't remember all of the traveling I've done, you see. I fade in and out of consciousness. Like today, when I woke up with my hands around your neck. I don't know where or who I had been in the moments before I came to."

But I knew. I knew only too well that the man who had tried to kill me wasn't the one sitting across from me now. The man who had tried to kill me was my own father.

"Does he talk to you, then?" I asked. "The other one?"

He shook his head.

"No, nobody talks to me. I just sort of get a feeling about things. Something's driving me to do these things, I can tell you that. Why else would anybody come to a place like this?" He looked around us at the sunburned hills, now gray in the twilight. "There's nothing here, is there?

Nothing except this gold." He reached into his pack and pulled out a small handful of smaller gold pieces, fingered through them as if amazed that anyone could care about something so silly. "But this...being...it wills me to go, and so I go. And like I said, sometimes I just wake up and I'm somewhere new. Like today."

Cait climbed up onto the wall next to me and rested her head on my shoulder. She gave a long, shuddering yawn. It seemed she had no ill feelings toward me for abandoning her below.

"I want to go home," she said, her voice sleepy now in the gathering darkness. "I want to see Rhainn-y." Then, she lifted her head and looked deep into my eyes. "You should believe him," she said. "I do."

I looked between her and the man who, despite his current condition, was my father.

I didn't know who to believe anymore.

But one thing was for certain. We now had enough gold to return to the Triaden. Enough to put it to good use. Maybe we would have a chance at success now. We could even end this thing if we were lucky. And maybe we *could* find Rhainn.

But still, I doubted.

"Who will take care of you?" I asked. "If we do go, there's a war, you know. And we don't even know if we'll find everyone from Stonemore where we left them."

"Lissa would take care of me," she said, bargaining.

'If we stay here, then my mom and Grandma could take you back to the farm. I bet you could watch all the television you wanted. Maybe you could even get to see Lily sometimes."

She thought about this. She had made a good connection with Mom, that was for sure. And the draw of Carl's young daughter was certainly appealing. But the draw back to her homeland, no matter how sick and overrun it was at the moment, was too strong for her.

"I want to be with Rhainn-y," she said quietly.

I sighed into the top of her head. I had brought her here to try to protect her from the madness of her worlds. But since our arrival, she had been anything but protected. Now, with her clearly voiced desire to return back to her one chance at having what was left of her family back by her side again, I felt helpless to deny her.

Finally, I gave in.

"Okay," I said. "We can try."

I looked up at my father, who hadn't voiced an opinion one way or the other about this course of action.

"What about you?" I asked. "What will you do?"

It had been my intention to take him with us when we did finally go back. But now everything had changed.

"I'll go where you go," he said. "If you'll have me."

I swallowed heavily, my throat still sore from his earlier attack. He seemed to know my mind.

"I'm sorry about what happened before," he said. "I don't know if I can convince you, but I have no desire to hurt you."

"No," I said. "It's my father that wants to do that."

And for this, like so many other things, he had no explanation.

"It's alright," I said. And something in his manner, something in the kind way those black eyes looked at me, made the decision for me. "You can come."

The tiniest seed was planted deep in my heart, had taken root there long ago and refused to let go. There was still a chance. There was always a chance.

Maybe somewhere hidden deep inside this man I looked at now, my father still remained. Maybe the man who had fed me ice cream for the first time and pushed tiny train cars across the carpet of our city apartment was still in there. Somewhere.

# CHAPTER TWENTY-FIVE

As night fell around us in earnest, we set out to find somewhere comfortable to sleep. I showed him the museum, which he hadn't seen before, at least not in this state. To one side of the gift shop entry, a narrow staircase snaked up along the side of the building. He carried Cait, who had fallen asleep, up the stairs, where a shopkeeper's apartment was built above the main structure. He gently lay her sleeping body down onto a small couch on the far side of the room, taking care to remove her bulky helmet before he did so. Then, with a tenderness I did not expect, he bent down over her and kissed her gently on the forehead, smoothing out her ratty hair with one hand.

I slumped into a big cushy armchair, exhausted. I slid my backpack around to my front and opened it, stuffing the large gold stone into it. My fingers brushed up against Brendan's diary, which I hadn't read since before Denver. By the light of the headlamp, I flipped it open at random.

*March 21, 1899*

*I am trying to keep true to my original purpose here, but the struggles of everyday life are enough to sometimes make me forget the importance of my quest. I have gathered so little gold, and seen so little magic, that I fear I may never be able to return home. And yet, I must press on. I must not give up the fight, no matter how difficult it may become to continue.*

*Sometimes I am tempted to tell Josephine, to enlist her to help me in some way that I cannot yet imagine. But the fear that she may see madness where there is truth stops me from enlightening her. The dust fire does not come at all anymore, and if I were to try to prove my stories it would accomplish little but making me look a fool. I fear not appearing foolish, but her trust is something I value dearly, and I do not want to scare her.*

*So I continue on, on my own, in secret. It is all I can do. It is the best I can do. I hope that one day I will be able to prove the truth of my past to her, or that her trust in me will be so great that I will be able to tell it to her frankly.*

*Until then, the search continues in solitary fashion. For the gold. For the magic that was once so close to me it felt as a brother. Though both have eluded me for many years, I push forward in the hope that one day the spark of power will ignite from my fingertips once more.*

I read the passage over and over, certain that there was something within it that might help me find my way out of the darkness. But all was a foggy mess in my brain, my heart. I looked up to find my father sitting across from me in a matching armchair, gazing at me with curiosity. I raised my eyebrows at him.

"What is our plan?" he asked. His manner was mild. His face friendly. Yet still I tried to avoid looking into his eyes.

I turned off my headlamp and tucked the diary back into my

backpack, sitting across from him in the dark to spare me the pain of seeing all that black.

"Tomorrow I'll take you to the Fold, I think," I said.

"Oh," he said. "What is that?"

I let my head rest against the arm of the chair, too exhausted to try to stay up and watch him. A large yawn escaped me despite my effort to appear alert.

"It's a place," I said. "A place where we might be able to heal you."

"But what is wrong with me?" he asked. "I don't feel ill."

"Yes," I said. "That's always sort of been the whole problem."

"The girl is coming, too?" he asked. In the light of the moon coming through the small window, I saw him turn and look in Cait's direction. "That is what you want?"

"Yes," I said, thinking that I would be hard pressed to deny her.

"Good," he said. "There's something about her. Something I like."

I turned and looked over at Cait, too, her little body curled up into a ball on the couch. She seemed so content, as if nothing more dramatic than a rough day of play had just passed her by. I marveled at her resilience, her ability to remain steadfast in her wants and dreams despite all the mayhem that had surrounded her for so long. Perhaps there was more to her magic than just following trails and connecting people with their desires. Perhaps the power of Elyso had bestowed other, less obvious, gifts as well.

I opened my mouth to speak when a low rumbling snore came from him. It appeared that the day's events had tired every one of us out.

I turned back to Cait, watched her light breathing as she slipped into a dreamland all her own. I made a wish for her that it was full of brightness tonight, that fear and angst stayed far away from her mind as she rested.

"I like her, too," I whispered.

At the sound, my father tucked his arms into his chest and rolled onto one side, sleeping as soundly as a child.

I let my own head rest against the arm of my chair, and when I closed my eyes, I remembered the blackness of the cave as it had been punctuated by the pinpricks of stars across my vision. I remembered the huge swaths of stars I had seen when I had been on the snow planet staring out, wishing to see some hint of home. Of here. And it was with that as my backdrop, the galaxies that represented all life, that I finally let myself fall into sleep.

We jumped through the next morning and most of the afternoon without rest, he taking this new mode of travel easily in stride. We rarely stopped, rarely walked, rarely slept. It seemed that all of us were eager to leave this place, now that we had the gold we needed and the decision had been made. During one of the brief rests we did take, he dug out the rest of the gold he had discovered, including the snarl of necklaces from the attic.

"Don't know where these came from," he said, handing them to me. "But I worked for weeks to get this." He passed over a small vial, and inside floated gold specks similar to those I had carried with me since Colorado. I took his giving me all of these as a gesture of trust, and I tried to listen to the small voice inside my head that told me the Corentin, himself would never give away all his gold like this.

It was strange, but now that we were together, I felt as alone as I had that first instant I had jumped to the Fold from the attic. Nothing was turning out to be what I had thought it was, and my understanding of truth was no longer what I had believed. I craved the contact of my friends, of the people in the Triaden who had helped me so much along this journey. I wanted to trust Dad, and there were moments when I was thrust back into the mind of a young child, looking up to him, believing him.

But each time those black eyes stared back at me, the trust faded away, and I was left alone again.

Only Cait, who seemed happier now than I had ever seen her, kept me moving forward. She was excited to see Larissa again, and I think maybe she thought Rhainn would somehow appear before us upon our arrival back in the Fold. Either way, it was a relief to not have to drag her along, and her energy lifted all of us as we faced the arduous journey back to the countryside, back to the spot in the land where the chaser's magic would take us all across the universe in a reverse trip.

When we finally did start to see the remains of the land on the other side of the Rockies, the decimated cornfields, the houses slowly melting back into the Earth, I was relieved. The sun was high in the sky, and the clouds were still far off on the horizon, not yet ready to threaten the land below.

Finally, as we jumped through the fields near the strange rock formations that had served as my marker, I knew we were close. Soon, we landed on a spot not far from a small cluster of buildings, too far away to see clearly, but close enough to look familiar. I couldn't tell for sure, but it was as likely to be the old farmhouse as any structures we might find still standing out this way. I felt certain that, here, we were close enough to our original entry point to use the chaser successfully.

I strained my eyes, looking for signs of life, half hoping to hear the shouts of protest of my mother commanding me to stay home. I saw very little, though, and from here the tiny lump that sat beside the house might have been the old sedan we had ridden in across our wrecked country, or could have been nothing more than a boulder deposited here millions of years ago.

She didn't come running. Nobody saw us appear.

Nobody would see us leave.

I looked up into my father's face, so benign and weirdly friendly. He smiled down at me.

I had to figure him out. Who this man who stood before me now really was. That body, those hands, had tried to snuff out my life yesterday. And now he stood before me, as agreeable as could be despite the grip that clearly held him, rendering his memory blank and his actions gentle. I might have chosen the safer path, to leave him behind. The risk of bringing him hung heavily over me. I could have pushed on alone in my quest to rectify the imbalance of the Fold with one less uncertain ally by my side. But if I did, the mystery of what had happened to my father would haunt me forever. Keeping him close could be my only chance to discover the truth before I succeeded, or failed, in my mission. The truth about what had happened to him.

And about how he really felt about me.

I stared out across the land, hoping it was not for the last time. In my mind, I made the promise I knew I might not be able to keep.

*Meet you back here, Mom.*

Then, I turned my back from the place, and knelt to dig into the old backpack for the chaser. My hand closed around it, and I realized that now it reminded me of something in recent memory: one of the hard, smooth balls from the pool table where Cait and I had learned to play.

I smiled, relishing the feeling of its cool surface against my palm.

Then I held it out, and the gold floating within it winked in the late afternoon sun. I took Cait's hand in mine, and she took my father's in her other.

Then, with one last look up into the acid sky, we left this place.

My planet.

My world.

My home.

One of the most helpful things you can do for any author is to leave an honest review. Please leave a review!

Mother of two, horse enthusiast, and serial entrepreneur, J. B. Cantwell calls the San Francisco Bay Area home. In the Aster Wood series, she explores coming of age in an imperfect world, the effects of greed and violence on all, and the miraculous power that hope can have over the human spirit.

Made in the USA
Middletown, DE
12 August 2016